In The Land of Cotton

Maryann Austin

Copyright Maryann Austin 2013

Wila Publishing

ISBN 978-0615735818
1st edition.

Dedicated to my strong and kind husband,
Bill Austin

Special thanks to Jennifer Lickey and Billy Muse of
Capon Bridge, WV

Preface

A cannon boomed, sending a feeling of shock through the men, already in the midst of mayhem and blood. Throughout the smoky crowd, soldiers paired off, one against another, as close to the enemy as one can get. Face to face, a good many of them killed or met their deaths. And so it happened time and again. It happened to young men and it happened to boys…and, at times, it happened to others.

Chapter One

"Get up, boy! Get up!"

The young soldier huddled on the ground, shaking as shotgun blasts engulfed him. Sobbing into his sleeve, he shielded his face from the overwhelming light and noise. "God, I want to go home. Please let me go home." Hot lead burned inside his leg.

"Boy, get up! I tell you, get up!"

In the darkness and confusion, arms grabbed him around the middle and moved him. His mind was in a panic, but his body was limp. He imagined his mother coming for him and stealing him away to safety, out of this hell.

A voice gentler than the Lieutenant's spoke into his ear, and he found himself being taken farther into the woods and away from the skirmish. "C'mon boy. Don't worry. C'mon." His panic settled some. Images of his mother flitted around his mind. Yes, it was surely the voice of a woman. And he felt her touch. Tiredness overcame him and he drifted off as warm crimson blood drained from a nicked artery.

"What do you think you're doing? Look at 'im! He's no good to us in that condition." The Lieutenant yelled at his subordinate, bending so he would be heard. "You would a done better to leave him be. He'd be resting in a better place by now if you knew how to mind your own business!"

The soldier replied, "His daddy might feel differently, sir."

"Well, I ain't his daddy. And he'd a been nothing more than a sad story by now if you'd a left 'im! Now he's a burden to this Company. You refrain from such meddling in the future, boy. Cover your own behind!"

The soldier stared back, but didn't speak.

"Am I understood?"

Silence was returned.

"I *said*, am I understood?!

The soldier finally replied, "Yes, sir."

"Now he's *your* problem. You stay low out here, and pray you don't get separated. If anything happens, it ain't *my* failing." He retreated into the sound of gunfire and the orange flashes of light.

The soldier crouched in the darkness, cradling the wounded child's head and squeezing his hand. Surely his mama and daddy would want that. For he wouldn't see another sunrise, and it seemed the right thing, to offer comfort in a child's last hours on earth--no matter how hellish a place he was lucky to be leaving. Loudly, and unheard by anyone but the dying boy, the soldier sang:

I got a home in glory land that outshines the sun
I got a home in glory land that outshines the sun
I got a home in glory land that outshines the sun
Way beyond the blue

And by and by the boy's hand lost its warmth, and the soldier didn't sing anymore that night. The dead boy was lain in a position that made him look like he was sleeping. And he was left there where he died.

When the sun rose, a dozen or so bodies were visible scattered about the field and woods. Different shapes and sizes, but all with one thing in common. Fighting for a cause yesterday, dead today. Some soldiers meandered in a daze. Others more purposeful, bending every so often to examine the dead. Comrade or enemy, it didn't matter. For the dead don't need belongings. So their pockets would be scavenged, and their army-issued canteens and weapons would be collected as souvenirs or put to good use. Sometimes, a scavenger would get lucky and find something to eat in the pockets of the dead. And on this morning, Private Jacob Burdock had such fortune. At his feet lay a dead Union devil. Fittingly the colors of the flag: red hair, pasty white face, and eyes open in an icy blue stare.

Burdock hocked his throat and spat down toward the corpse in anger. "I don't believe I like the way you're looking at me, brother."

From experience, he could quickly scan a dead man and have a good idea if there was anything worth taking. This one's jacket lay open, revealing his belly and the top of his pants. Burdock spotted an unnatural-looking bulge protruding from the right pocket. He plunged his hand inside. The body was cold, but he was damned if that biscuit didn't still feel warm. "Well, this must be my lucky day," he said to himself. He spat again for good measure and sauntered away, satisfied with the findings of the morning. "Hey! Hey you!" He called out to a group of men. "Bet yer hungry! See what I got here! You survived last night's bullets, but you probly ain't gonna survive the starvation!"

He made his way closer to the men. No one looked at him, because they had known him to be a smell fungus. But that didn't stop him. He approached anyway, still ranting loudly. "That dead boy's the lucky one. Yes, he is. He won't have to starve out here." The others ignored him, sickened and too worn out to be bothered.

With reproach, he said, "You men think you're so high 'n mighty. You're too *good* to take from dead men." He yelled now, covering them with a fine mist of spittle. "Well, being good ain't gonna do you *no* good when you're good and *DEAD*." He continued past them mumbling. "You wait an' see whose dead and whose alive at the end. You wait an' see."

When he was far enough away that they knew he wasn't coming back, the soldiers talked about him. "That's a crazy man right there." They all nodded in agreement.

The men surveyed one another. There were no mirrors, so one could only judge himself by what he saw in others. Thin and dirty. Thin and dirty. Everyone was the same. Some were caked with blood, too.

"Is that your blood, or some poor fool's blood?"

The soldier answered in a deep voice, "It's the boy's blood."

"Mmmmhmmm. He's not around this morning, is he?"

Pointing toward the trees, the soldier responded, "He's over there. He died."

Another spoke up. "The Lieutenant said you weren't right in the head." Several looked at him with ire for repeating the offending words. But he continued. "He said you risked your life, and ours, for a dead boy. He said that you're watering down our fightin' spirit."

"I don't intend to water down your spirit."

In a jovial tone, another added, "He's already drank all our water! Now he's tryin' to take our spirits too?!"

Stupid laughter erupted and echoed eerily over the carnage.

"Alright men!" The Lieutenant walked briskly closer.

"We need to move before the heat of the day sets in. The smell of death is strong!" He shouted at the men and waved his arms for them to rise and gather their things, repeating, "the smell of death is strong!" Today the already-small Company was down to eleven live souls. And those who remained collected whatever worldly possessions they had and formed a sorry-looking line. "March men!"

For two hours they marched and the sun rose higher in the sky. The foliage of the woods kept them shaded, but mosquitoes and gnats buzzed around their salty faces. Some let the bugs fly into their mouths, and then consumed them. It provided satisfaction to swallow anything other then their own spit. A few of the men had even eaten worms and grubs, trying to quiet shrunken bellies.

In time, the bugs became worse. Mosquitoes bit the ears, necks, and hands of the men. When they slapped the pests against themselves, the Lieutenant yelled, "Harder! Are you women?! Harder!" Many of them scratched until blood leaked out, and the initial bites were no longer visible.

Somebody reached into their pocket. "I was saving this." He pulled out a crushed homemade cigar. Examining it, he fluffed it a little and pulled a piece of flint from his other pocket. Soon the itchy soldiers were closing in on him, seeking some relief. The soldier bent down and set the cigar on the ground while he searched for a rock. He struck the flint against it until it sparked. Then he lit a dry leaf and transferred the flame to the cigar. He began to puff, savoring the flavor, and imagining that it could actually fill his concave belly. He blew his smoke into their faces, a gesture that would be insulting during normal times. But it was a welcome one now. For it would keep the flying pests away--at least for a while.

One young soldier stood alone outside the circle.

"C'mon, boy. Don't tell me that you prefer the bite of skeeters to a little smoke."

Still scratching, the soldier answered. "Smoke steals my breath, sir."

Burdock chimed in roughly, "There's a lot worse than smoke that'll steal your breath out here, boy!" He grabbed the young man and shoved him toward the others. The young soldier went down on his hands and knees. Trying to conceal his embarrassment, he quickly rose and brushed the dirt off his elbows and knees.

"Men, that's enough now," the Lieutenant said. He looked at the one with the cigar, "sir, I would be obliged if I could take the last few drags from that smoke." His words sounded like a request, but they were more of a demand. He took the cigar, inhaling and puffing. "This tastes like shit." He laughed sarcastically and continued inhaling, savoring the taste. Anything was better than the rotten breath of starvation. He continued until the cigar was gone. Dropping the useless tip to the ground, he angrily mashed it in with his boot heel. He gestured for his men to follow, and they resumed their walk.

There were times that the Lieutenant preferred silence. One would think that it was because he was listening for the enemy, but it was usually just because the sound of talking irritated him. He preferred the sounds inside his mind, and the sounds of his own gas and belching. And he could hear neither while the fools yammered. Today, though, maybe because of the cigar, he seemed less touchy--so unbothered, the men talked amongst themselves as they walked.

Soldiers paired off and conversed about things that reminded them of home and the normal lives they left behind. "You got a girl back home?" one asked another.

The reply was sheepish. "No." The soldier seemed uncomfortable with the question.

Jokingly, the other retorted, "You like boys or somethin'?"

Avoiding eye contact, Cotton stared ahead, not answering.

"Oh, c'mon, Cotton. Just havin' a little fun with ya." He added quietly, talking from the side of his mouth. "Ya know, I don't keer what the tenant says, it were an admirable thing you did for that dead boy."

The other nodded, reminded of the fallen child. "I was just doing what was right."

"Mmmm. Right. Wrong." Talking now to himself, he

looked straight ahead. "I used to know that killin' a man was wrong. But now, damned if I don't wonder if it's right sometimes." He almost whispered. "I mean, it couldn't be right to spare somebody else if it cost my own life. Could it?" He looked at his companion searching for an answer.

"I couldn't presume to tell you. I haven't been faced with that situation, and I hope never to be." He reached up toward a bug-bitten chin and scratched.

"I have a girl back home."

Cotton listened.

"She's kind-hearted. What you did last night, she would a done too. But I guess that's more to be expected, her bein' a girl."

Cotton shrank with discomfort.

"Don't worry, man. I ain't callin you a girl." He went on. "Her name's Daphna. She's pretty. Long yellow hair. Shines like the sun. I can't wait to smell that pretty hair again." Without warning, his excitement turned to frustration, as if struck with the realization that he might not see her again.

Cotton looked at him briefly, then resumed a forward stare. The talking ended and the walking continued. The sun was hotter now, and dryness settled into their throats. Their thoughts turned to the next wet creek bed where canteens could be filled and thirsts could be quenched.

In the quiet, blurry memories danced in Cotton's mind.

Sweet honeysuckle filled the air. Hand in hand, a boy and a girl walked together. Smiling at one another, they exchanged the innocent kisses of youth. From his pocket, the boy produced a locket on a necklace. And he placed it on her. She ran her fingers back and forth on the chain. For she had never owned real jewelry before, and certainly nothing like this. To her young heart, it was a delight. She buried her face into his warm chest and they embraced. She savored him, drawing in his essence through her mouth and nostrils.

The gruff voice of the Lieutenant ended the dream. "Water, men! And if anyone has other business to tend to, do it now! We need to reach the encampment before nightfall!" The men unbuckled their canteens and rushed to the trickling stream. They lowered themselves to the muddy bank and splashed refreshing coolness to burned and itchy faces.

Cotton plunged his hands into the cool water and rubbed. He removed the blood that had been caked on since the night before, glad to be rid of its thick stickiness. Glad to be rid of such a reminder. When his hands were clean, he splashed his smooth young face. To the exhausted soldiers, the icy water was like a stimulant. When done washing and drinking, they all felt a little more awake, a little more alive. And when they resumed their march, they moved with a little more purpose.

Chapter Two

Boone, North Carolina is a place where the snow flies early on the mountain. Most years, it would be October when the five Cotton children would have kissed the summer goodbye and watched icicles form on the banks of the New River. People were strong there, and the Cottons were no different. They had the distinction of being the only family in town whose children were all living. All five: three boys and two girls. In the years before the war, life was different…but not *that* different.

"Zebediah! What have you done now?" Mrs. Cotton ushered her eldest child to the table and brushed the hair from his face. "Boy, who have you been fightin' with?"

He looked down in shame and replied quietly. "Josiah Jackson, ma'am." His lip was busted open, and a gob of bloody spit dripped from his mouth.

Mrs. Cotton grabbed a cloth from a nail on the wall and cleaned his face. "What business do you have with Josiah

Jackson?"

Embarrassed and angry, he replied, "He's been foolin' with my sister."

"Your sister," she confirmed, lowering her chin and raising one eyebrow.

"Yes, ma'am. Della. He's been messin' with Della."

"I see. Well, you never mind that boy anymore." She brushed his shoulders and shooed him away from the table. "You go find Della and send her to me. You tell her Momma wants to speak to her." He knew what that meant.

It was Mrs. Cotton's custom to appear calm. But it gave no comfort to Zebediah, sure that he just bought his sister a whipping with a willow switch. And Della would have to pay for the sins of that horny boy. Zeb knew his sister. Innocent and sweet as an angel. It wasn't her fault that wolves like Josiah Jackson tried to take advantage of her. *Poor Della* he thought.

Over the big stepping stones in the river, he took a shortcut to where he knew she would be. Sitting in the middle of a cool and bare field. She often went there to feed a stray dog. Bringing him old biscuits and an occasional scrap of some kind of meat, the sort that not even mountain people would eat. Coming closer, Zebediah slowed his pace. He saw the dog, and the dog saw him. At twenty feet away, he called. "Della! Momma wants you! Come home! Momma wants to see you!" He stepped closer, and the dog growled, rising to his feet--or whatever dogs rise to. Zeb shuddered and calmly backed away, trying to conceal his fear.

Della scratched the dog under the chin, calling him off the interloper. "It's alright boy. Don't worry. C,mon." She led him in the opposite direction, toward the woods. The dog felt safe there. It was where he stayed when not visiting his one human friend. Comprehending, he did as he was instructed. But he turned around and gave one last warning growl, then dashed into the thicket.

"What does Momma want now?" she asked.

He couldn't tell her that Momma knew about Josiah. So he replied, "Beats me."

Della and Zebediah Cotton walked home to their clapboard house. Knowing what was coming, Zeb remained outside, gritting his teeth as his unsuspecting sister stepped inside the door. He heard the familiar discord, the crack of a willow switch on the table. It was a sound he knew well--a sure sign that something worse was coming. Unable to bear it, he turned and ran. He ran as fast as he could. Back to the place where his sister sat petting a dog moments before. There he could pretend that it wasn't happening.

In his mind, Della still sat there petting that mongrel that made her so happy. He imagined she wasn't laying bare-bottomed across the table they ate on. He imagined that she was not being whipped bloody by someone they called *mother*.

But she was. And in a few short minutes it was over. Exhausted, Mrs. Cotton tucked her loose shirt back into her apron and struggled to catch her breath. "That will teach you to mess with boys. I ain't gonna raise no harlot. Now make yourself decent and leave me be."

"Yes." She purposely omitted *Ma'am.* And as instructed, she left. Her chin quivered under a straight face and she calmly walked away--away from that house. Della was a wise and experienced child, and she knew how to put her thoughts elsewhere. She knew how to escape the anguish. Envisioning the dog and his soft fur, she kept her mind on him now. Not on her stinging backside.

As Della thought of him, he patrolled the edge of his woods. He had paced back and forth there often enough that a worn path served as a boundary defining the space in which he might tolerate you from where he would surely kill you.

His ears and his nose were keen. And an approaching figure in the distance gave him cause to turn his head. Stopping his march, he stood facing an unwelcome guest.

Zebediah plopped down onto the scratchy dry weeds. Guilt for what he had done to his sister weighed heavily. He sat cross-legged and stared at the ground. Taking it all out on a blade of grass, he shredded it into tiny pieces. Every minute or so he looked up, watching for Della, needing to see her and know that his mother hadn't killed her.

The dog, too, watched. *Who is this interloper?* He tried to pick up on a scent, creeping closer. This was not his trusted friend. Some unknown smell. And the animal was on guard. He had learned that, except for the kind girl, all humans were enemies and not to be trusted. Even the smallest ones had brought harm to him, pelting him with rocks as they shouted. The bigger ones fired guns in his direction as he ran for his life.

Alerted by a sound behind him, Zebediah turned. And before he could even yell, the dog was on him. The animal had the advantage. For its prey was already down. So it bounded at him over and over again, drooling and growling as it snapped small pieces of flesh off of his arms.

Flailing bleeding limbs, Zebediah punched at his attacker. He kept his arms up, protecting his head and neck. And he continued to swing as the dog snapped at him. "Get off me you damn stupid animal!" But the dog clamped his jaw on the boy's hand, piercing it in a tight grip. Panic stricken, Zeb thought that the dog might be winning. And sensing imminent surrender, the animal released the hand and targeted Zebediah's back and neck while his prey cowered, screaming.

"Rogue, No!" Della ran toward the scene. Frenzied, the animal did not acknowledge her, but continued his attack. He inflicted two more good bites before he was yanked off of his victim. Still operating on adrenaline and instinct, he turned toward Della, bit down hard into her arm and jerked away. A moment later a familiar scent registered in his canine brain.

"Stop, boy, stop." She spoke soothingly to calm him, then took his face in her two hands. Looking into his eyes, she gritted her teeth and took the role of the alpha. "No! Don't you ever do that again! Now *go!*" She shoved his face away from her and the dog was ashamed. He ran toward the woods with his tail between his legs, head lowered. And he did not look back.

Zebediah lay on the ground, crying and choking on his own spit.

"Zeb. Zeb. It's alright now. He's gone. I'm so sorry."

Her brother offered no answer, embarrassed and ashamed of his tears. Della ran toward the stream. She plunged her skirt into the cold water and drenched it. She returned swiftly to Zebediah.

Wiping her brother's injuries, she examined him to assess the damage. She moved his hair to the side. Bloody scratches were visible on the back of his neck. Blood streamed from multiple gashes on his arms. She cleaned his wounds and surveyed the rest of him. "Is there anything else, Zeb? Did he get you anywhere else?"

He sat up and reached toward her, revealing a badly damaged hand. It quivered as he lifted it for her to see. *Holes in a person were a dangerous thing.* It was not uncommon in those days for a person to die from such a wound. And the girl knew that it would have to be cleaned quickly. She knew nothing of germs, but acted on instinct.

Della led her brother to the water and put in his hand. He held it down while she gently rubbed it under the water, washing away blood, dirt, and dog saliva. As the shock began to wear off for Zeb, the pain settled in. And the young girl reassured him. "Don't worry, Zebediah. You'll be alright."

She searched around for something with which to cover the bite. "Give me your shirt." He obliged, handing it over to her, trying not to use the injured hand too much. She tied it firmly to stop the bleeding.

"Not so tight!"

"Shhhh." She put her arm around his back and led him over the stepping stones and homeward.

Della was younger than Zeb, but she was like a mother to him in tense situations. Though she was young, somehow she knew what to say. Somehow she knew what to do to make things better. And she was also wise enough to know when there was no hope for a good outcome.

In this instance, though, she had a feeling that her brother would survive his injuries. The greater threat might be the wrath of their mother. She had warned all of them to stay away from strange animals. Mrs. Cotton made it clear that possums, squirrels, goats, and (yes) even dogs were for eating. Not for children's play. She counted them no different from the farm animals that the wealthier people dined on.

23

Closer to home, Mary came running. The youngest of the Cotton children, her face was always covered in sideways boogers. For her treatment of a runny nose was an arm swipe that left a horizontal snot across her face. So, boogery and excited to see her older siblings, she scurried happily toward them. But when she saw the bandaged hand, her countenance quickly changed.

"Momma's gonna keel you." She announced it with concern, and not brattiness. "I heard what you done to Josiah Jackson. Oh, Momma's gonna keel you, Zeb."

Della spoke up, "*What* did you do to Josiah Jackson?"

"He shouldn't be foolin' with you, Dell." He paused, trying to work up enough courage to continue. "And it ain't right for you to be foolin' with him either!"

Angry, she replied. "It's not your place tell me who to be *foolin'* with, Zeb!" She looked him in the eye. "Did you hurt him?"

"Whatever I did to him, he deserved. I hope he wears that badge of shame over his eye for a fortnight."

"And, thanks to my brother, I'm wearin' my own badge of shame," she growled back.

Remorseful, Zebediah looked down.

Della walked toward the house, calling back to him, "You better let Momma dress that." And she walked away.

Mrs. Cotton lovingly tended to her son's injuries. There

24

seemed no rhyme or reason to his mother's reactions. But he was grateful that she spared the willow switch. He had been whipped for less. And he went to bed that night feeling lucky. His hand was the size of a cannonball, and it hurt like hell, but his behind and his pride were still in tact. It had been a rough day for Mrs. Cotton--and one beating was certainly enough.

Chapter Three

When Cotton and the rest of the Company reached the field encampment somewhere south of Lexington, it was already past nightfall. In the dark, small groups clustered around fires. "Men, welcome to your accommodations. Make yourselves at home." In seconds, his dark image blended with the night, and he could be seen no more.

Because they were newcomers, and because the men already there numbered in the dozens, they were intimidated. Except for Burdock, they stayed close to one another as they made their way in, seeking acceptance--and perhaps some food.

Cotton spotted someone close to his own young age and crouched down next to him. "I'm Zebediah Cotton from Boone, North Carolina."

"Evening, Zebediah. You'll find corn bread in that bucket. I'd be surprised you can find more salt pork, but go ahead 'n try. If there ain't no more here, I'd go yonder and see."

He pointed to the next small group gathered around their own fire.

"Thank you," Cotton replied.

With their equipment still on their backs, the newcomers helped themselves to the dry food, not caring how desperate or hungry they appeared. Such behavior would have been frowned upon at the supper table. But the comfort and judgment of the supper table had been left behind.

No one talked. They just ate. They chewed and savored the food and filled their shrunken bellies. And when there was no more, they sat for a good while and lost themselves in the glow of the campfire.

From behind them a voice directed, "Don't be staring into that fire all night. Confuses the eyes, makin' you a easy target. You put that thing out soon."

They did as they were instructed and, in seconds, sizzling smoke and blackness surrounded them. With no further reason to sit up, they laid out their bedrolls. All were exhausted. Some slept. Some could not. Cotton lay there in the quiet, more comfortable than he had been the night before. But not very.

"Cotton! Cotton! Over here!" A few bodies away, a voice called to him. He recognized it. It was the young soldier at the fire.

"Will you come with me? I have to take a piss. Will you come with me before I burst open?"

Reluctantly, Cotton agreed. The other boy was young enough to be afraid of ghosts. And, when you're in a war there's more than ghosts of the imagination to fear. The fire had left blind spots on their eyes, and Cotton followed the boy who knew where he was going. The sound alerted him that his company was relieving himself, and he shyly looked away.

"You gonna go?"

Embarrassed, he answered, "No."

"Ashamed uh yer manhood?"

Cotton remained silent.

Pulling his britches up, the boy mumbled, "I couldn't see nothing if I tried." He added a warning. "Don't ask me to go witcha later."

"I don't even know your name. And you want me to take a pee in front of..."

The boy answered, "I guess you *would* expect to know somebody before peein' in front of em. I'm Cumfrey. Private John Cumfrey. 18th North Carolina Infantry, Company B." Considering the darkness, and what he had just used his hand for, he did not offer a handshake.

They walked back to their makeshift beds and lay down.

Cumfrey asked. "How long?"

"How long what?" Cotton asked.

They continued in whispers.

"How long you been in the army?"

"I left Boone the end of April."

"Damn. Yer just a infant. I been in this hell for three months now." He paused. "I swear it feels like a year."

"Where's your home?" Cotton inquired.

Sarcastically, he said, "*Home.* I was born and raised in Bladen County. I wouldn't call it home, though."

"I miss Boone."

Cumfrey retorted, "Well I don't miss Bladen County." He lowered his voice even more now, so no one else would hear. "They made me come. I don't keer who owns slaves and who don't. I don't keer about none of this session mumbo jumbo."

"Would you rather have turned on your brothers in South Carolina?"

"They's my *brother* as much as any *yankee*'s my brother. I wasn't about to let *nobody's* president tell me to march into South Carolina."

Cotton remained silent and let John talk.

"The bastards made me come. Diggs and Henry." Though it was dark, he looked around to make sure they weren't close by. "Said they was gonna shoot my dog and string me up if I didn't go like a man." He shook his head in disgust.

Clyde Diggs and Caleb Henry had grown up with John. The three knew each other well. As young boys, they fished the same streams and swam the same ponds. There was no ill will between them. And when North Carolina seceded from the

29

Union, they spent many evenings together, sitting around a fire, sharing tales about how they would join the Infantry and kill as many yankee devils as possible. But to John, it was just talk.

The war brought strife, and there were food riots in Bladen County. The trouble sparked a fire under Diggs and Henry. And they figured if they were going to die of starvation, they would do it as men, killing the damn yanks who were responsible for ending life as it had been known in the south.

"Dog's probly dead now anyways." He looked down and sniffled.

It seemed like the boy was done, so Cotton spoke. "I have a dog." Blood and growling flashed in his mind.

John nodded and added, "I like dogs."

"I like my dog better than I like most people," said Cotton. "My mama don't care for animals. She says they're for eating. Dogs too."

"Well, I believe I might eat one right now!" They quietly laughed.

Cotton added, "sometimes I think it would be better to leave the dogs and eat the people."

"I believe I might could eat one of those too!"

They laughed again. They couldn't see in the darkness, but both were smiling. It was the first time in a while that either had done that. Under a cool spring sky they fell asleep, less alone than the night before.

As morning broke, many of the men went about the day's business. Rations ran out quickly, and if you wanted to eat, you'd better get up early. Cotton looked around, as if searching. Seeing the camp in daylight for the first time, he surveyed the area. In the dark of night, his mind filled the blanks. But now in the morning sun, he saw the reality of it. There were many more men than he had imagined. Probably two hundred strong. At least a fourth of them were smooth-faced and young like Cotton and Cumfrey.

For all of the movement, it was surprisingly quiet. More quiet than one might imagine it to be in the presence of so many men. A young boy approached.

The unfamiliar face said, "Whatcha starin at, Cotton?"

He knew the voice and replied, "Mornin' John."

John tossed a greasy piece of cornbread. "Here you go, friend."

In the midst of many soldiers, they felt both connected and removed. The unpleasant odor of unwashed men and their trench mouth stinking breath was something to which both had become accustomed. So, they sat and choked down their meal, ignoring the stench around them.

John rose. "C'mon!"

"C'mon where?" asked Cotton.

"You'll see." Getting impatient now. "C'mon!"

"Shouldn't we wait here?"

He replied, "Wait here for what?! There ain't nothing to do but sit around bored and hungry 'til we march agin! C'mon."

Seeing no Lieutenant or other superior, Cotton relaxed and moved about freely with his friend. For the first time since leaving Boone, he escaped the worry of looming danger. And walking with his new friend, he almost forgot about the war.

John led the way up a hillside. Stopping to catch his breath, Cotton spotted the river. Not just a muddy stream. It was a crystal fresh river like in Boone. The two ran to it and instinctively splashed cold water onto their faces. They drank, swishing the water around dry mouths before swallowing. John reached down and splashed his friend. Cotton returned fire. And the two laughed.

"C'mon," John ordered again.

Cotton followed, walking upstream along the riverside. They walked for a minute or so and they stopped short, staring ahead and upward. John stretched with his hands at his lower back. Cotton's jaw fell in wonderment.

Before them towered a bridge of rock. It must have been put there by God Himself. And the river flowed underneath it, right through the middle.

"C'mon. I got sumthin else to show ya," John urged.

Cotton did as he was told. They climbed a steep embankment toward the massive structure. John knew the exact spot. And standing within ten feet of it, he led his companion in front of him and pointed.

"You see that there?"

Above them, scratched into the formation, the letters *GW*.

He continued. "You're looking at the nitials of George Washington himself." Though a Confederate, he announced this fact with pride. He had never been in such close proximity to something or someone so important--not since Chancellorsville anyway. And that he would just assume forget.

"He came here when he was a young man, before he was *The* George Washington."

When the amazement wore off, Cotton's attention turned to the river, where John waded ankle-deep in the cold water.

"What are you looking at?" Cotton called to his friend.

"C'mere." He waved his arms, beckoning.

John bent and retrieved a small something out of the water. Standing up, he opened his hand for his friend to see.

Not sure what to make of it, Cotton asked, "Marble?"

"That ain't no marble. That's a musket ball." It was perfectly round and shiny.

The two crouched and rummaged for more. They returned to camp with two fistfuls each. John knew where he was going. He led Cotton to a bucket near the supply tent and they dropped them all in. As they hit, the balls made a sound like hard-falling rain.

"Thank you, boys," a deep voice said.

"Yes, sir," both called back.

Chapter Four

A year before, the Cotton family was whole. And now
two members were missing. Mrs. Cotton no longer counted
herself so fortunate as to have all of her children. Zebediah was
gone and Della had run off, probably after that Jackson boy.

"I miss Zeb," young Samuel cried.

"I miss him too, child." Mrs. Cotton wiped her face with
her apron.

Little Mary picked feathers from the floor. "Is Dell ever
gonna come home, Momma?" she inquired.

"That'll be up to her, baby." She pulled feathers from the
dead chicken on her supper table. It was a good release of
frustration, yanking them hard and throwing them down. "You
stick those feathers in yer piller. Don't let me see you with them
dirty things in yer hair."

"Yes, Ma'am," the little girl replied.

Samuel stopped his crying long enough to ask, "Where is

Della, momma?"

And she was far away. Della crept quietly through some bushes and toward the water. Her lower belly had been aching for days--and now the blood came. Washing was imperative. The smell of her monthly would draw unwelcome attention. So, stealthily, she moved to the water and removed her clothes. Her build was slight and almost boyish. She peered around like a hunted animal, making sure that she wasn't being watched.

Moving quickly, she washed herself off with the freezing cold water. There was no time to dry in the sun, so she put her clothes back onto her wet body, feeling very itchy and praying that the flow would not be heavy. When she was no longer hiding, she walked away from the water and into the wide open sunshine.

Della and the James River moved in tandem as she headed downstream. She thought about Zebediah, and she thought about Josiah Jackson. She would find him. Somehow. Approaching a group of soldiers, she checked each face. "Mornin'," she greeted them.

They nodded. "Mornin'."

She didn't beat around the bush. "Any of you men know a Private Josiah Jackson?"

They looked at each other shaking their heads. One replied. "No, I can't say I know anyone named Jackson. The only Jackson I knowed of was Major General *Stonewall*

Jackson." He said the name with an official tone. "An he's dead thanks to yer little friend."

"Excuse me?"

"Yer little friend. What's his name? Humfrey?" He looked at the others for an answer. "Dumfrie? Cumfrey! That's it."

She looked at him with confusion.

"Don't tell me the little traitor didn't tell ya?" He went on. "You be sure an ask him bout it. That boy's not a poplar fella round here. You'd do better to stay way from that one. Otherwise, ya might git yerself hurt."

"I don't intend getting hurt, sir." The Cotton child walked away rubbing a tiny, smooth musket ball in her hand.

Weeks earlier, the 18th North Carolina Infantry was fighting the Union when the unthinkable happened. John and a few of the other less valuable soldiers often served as pickets, expendable soldiers who stayed ahead and kept watch for the enemy. They prided themselves on being the first in line, the brave first indicator of a feared army. They once apprehended a Union Drummer with a pocket full of glass musket balls. "They're just marbles," he said. But they knew better.

On a bloody day in early May, at the battle of Chancellorsville, the Confederacy celebrated a sweeping victory--and a crushing loss. As fate had it, Private John Cumfrey was assigned to lead the group of young pickets that day. Many hours passed in boredom. John's bladder ached, and he saw no issue with stepping away for a moment to relieve himself. But as bad luck would have it, it was as he peed that the younger boys, armed with muskets, were alerted by the sound of someone on horseback.

Without their leader, they looked at one another in perfect silence. Their eyes wide open, shifting to and fro, listening. They readied their weapons and faced the direction of the noise. Quietly, they called. "John! John! Somebody's comin!"

But their voices were drowned out by the sound of pee hitting dry leaves. It was as John pulled up his britches that he heard them.

"John! Someone's comin!"

Panicked, he stumbled out of the thicket in time to see a blur of forms out of the corner of his eye. "Sweet Jesus, ther Union! Fire! Fire!"

Every armed picket fired, and when the smoke cleared, Stonewall Jackson himself lay on the ground bleeding from his wounds. They treated him by sawing off one of his arms, which was buried with honor. The rest of him was lain to rest in Lexington a few days later, when he succumbed to his wounds. Since all of the boys fired, it was impossible to know who actually hit him. And the blame naturally went to the one who gave the order. So the name of *John Cumfrey* became despised. Some of the men privately talked about killing him. Could they have gotten away with it, it would already be done.

In the daylight, John felt safer. Spying Cotton, he called out, "Where you been? I been looking all over for ya!"

"I went for a walk to clear my mind," Cotton replied.

In jovial sarcasm, he answered, "*Clear yer mind.* You're a peculiar one, Cotton."

"I guess so."

A hard shove interrupted the conversation. John hit the ground on his left side, dust rising around him. Diggs and Henry sauntered away. "Dumb bastard. Lucky it wasn't worse!" Diggs said. He spat at the ground and continued away with his cohort.

John looked at his friend, his eyes welling up. He looked down and tears splashed the ground. "Fools. They's the whole reason I'm here. I never woulda done it if theyda left me in Bladen County! It never woulda happened."

Cotton decided not to ask John about the details of that day. It would be better left alone. Anyway, John would never knowingly hurt a fly. Whatever happened, it must have been an accident. All Cotton had heard was that Jackson was killed by his own. And, surely that couldn't have been on purpose.

Midday crept closer and the camp grew more alive. Since the death of General Jackson, morale was low. But the men now moved about with more energy. For within a day or two, most of the camp would be vacated and the troops would march north, where they anticipated food--and fighting. For the food, all they needed was their bellies. But for the fighting, more was in order.

Ammunition was perpetually low. But the Confederates were resourceful. When there was nothing left to fire, soldiers picked up stones. If the stones were too big to fit inside the musket, they were hurled in the direction of the enemy. More than one Union devil had been pelted in the head by a thrifty southerner. But currently, the Valley District of the Army of the Confederate States of America was hopeful that they would have enough ammunition to take them through the next battle, wherever that might be.

At the encampment, there was a certain Sgt Richard Duckworth. He hailed from Wythe County where he had worked in the Wythe shot tower, learning the art of making musket balls by dropping heated lead from the top of a tower and into a pool of water below. Here, God created a natural shot tower for the use of the Confederacy. And Duckworth put his expertise to work at the camp near the James River.

"Stand clear!"

Cotton and Cumfrey watched. The men at the top of the bridge dropped single globs of molten lead to the water below. They glowed orange as they fell, forming perfect round shots while still in flight.

"Listen!" Cumfrey told his friend. The fiery orbs sizzled when they hit the water. But to hear it, one had to listen closely.

Tsssss...

They listened in wonderment. They watched and listened for quite some time, and anxiously waited. When it was done, they collected the newly-formed ammunition from the water.

Chapter Five

"I seen you girl." In the dark, Burdock gripped Della. He wrapped his right arm tightly around her and dug his hand into her shoulder. Struggling to get away, she stayed quiet. There were others close by, and she didn't want to draw unwanted attention.

"Where you going so soon?" He breathed his smelly hot breath into her ear.

"Let go!" she demanded in a forceful whisper, trying not to show her fear. She knew well that dogs could smell fear.

He licked the side of her face and she could feel his nasty rough tongue. She turned her head and spat toward him. Returning the gesture, he hocked into her face and threw her to the ground.

"Bitch!"

She leaned back on her hands and breathed hard. Her bottom jaw jutted out in disgust as she glared up at him.

"I'll kill you, whore!" He yelled in forceful whispers, displaying a shiny blade as proof. "I'm gonna keep yer little secret. Otherwise, you ain't no good to me. You won't get away with this, though."

Wiping the spittle from his face, he turned and walked back to camp.

Her body trembled in fear. And she sat in the dark, leaning against a maple tree. *How much longer could she keep up this pretense?* Burdock knew her secret. Maybe she would run away and try her luck on her own. yankees couldn't be any worse than him.

She buried her face in her hands, rubbing the spit away, gagging from the phlegmy grotesqueness of it.

Lord. Can You hear me? It's Della Cotton. I'm here in this war, Lord. I pray that You let evil men be repaid with evil. Protect me, and keep my brother Zeb. I ask that you help me to find Josiah Jackson. Help me to find him, and Your Will be done when I do. In Jesus' Holy Name I pray. Amen.

Her breathing calmed, and she gazed at the night sky. Many stars shone through the branches of the trees, twinkling in spite of the fighting and hatred on the earth. The wind blew gently, rustling the leaves overhead. And Della sensed that Burdock was far away. She rose, straightened her uniform, and quietly made her way back to the camp.

The fires burned late. Men savored the last night or two

of stability. Soon they would march and enter the unknown. And the unknown were a dangerous and frightening place to be. The farther north the less familiar. And the enemy could be anywhere at anytime.

In a person's own country, darkness isn't such a hindrance. But fighting in faraway places makes one an easy target--especially at night. So while still nestled in the land of cotton, Confederate soldiers gathered around glowing embers and caroused in the relative safety of the Confederacy. For in a few nights, they might be dead men.

Look away!

Look away!

Look away, Dixie Land!

The drunken chorus ended as Della approached, and it reminded her of home.

"Speakin' of Cotton!" one of them snorted. He gestured toward the soldier and cracked up at his own dumb joke.

Even the sober ones returned hearty drunken guffaws at the comment. Bored men are easily entertained. Doomed men want something to laugh about. So, from end to end, the camp was filled with merriment that night.

Lackawanna is the word that the native peoples use to describe where two rivers meet. About a hundred miles to the north and east of the camp at the natural bridge, the mighty Rappahannock meets the Rapidan. And there in a place called

Hartwood, a Brigade of three hundred gathered under the starlight near the small Yellow Chapel Church, preparing for a long march northward.

In this army, the Army of the Potomac, one would notice many more dark faces than would be found at the camp near the James River. There were a great many Negroes fighting for the Union--and honorably so. Some were born into freedom and others had been slaves who absconded from servitude, now considered *contraband* by the south. Wherever they came from, the Union Army welcomed them and put them to good use.

They were one with their white northern brothers, fighting alongside and for the same cause. All prayed to the same God as they marched in to battle. And still, around the individual campfires at night, white and brown stayed separate.

Funny, because if you were a fly sitting on the shoulder of any of those men, at any of those fires, you would hear the same hopes, and the same longings, and the same fears. War had a way of making everyone the same. And it whittled away at the unimportant. Any soldier--most anyway--found himself wishing for the simplest pleasures: to hold his child again, to feel the soft embrace of his woman again, to not have it occur to him that this night might be his last.

Oh God in heaven, how I would esteem these things if You would give them back to me. How many men had offered this prayer in time of war? Countless. Countless.

Chapter Six

Respect waned and fear grew as the soldiers of the Confederacy moved north. Each troop marched with his own Company, under his own Commanding Officer. The Regiment moved together in a loosely packed line, si-goggling' through the valley.

The Lieutenant rejoined his men. All of them appeared a little more rested and little less hungry. And even he felt a bit more human. Burdock knew the secret and Cotton worried. Maybe if she was lucky, he had been so drunk or tired that he just forgot. One thing was certain, she'd watch him more closely now. So unpleasant to look at, but she glanced at him more frequently than she had before.

Della preferred Burdock be in front of her, where she could keep an eye on him. But he marched behind. He looked her up and down and entertained bad thoughts about her. The look on his face was the usual hatred, so no one suspected anything. Whether he thought about taking a woman or killing a man, it all stirred up the same feelings. And he seemed to be wearing the same nasty mug no matter what. Della turned and looked behind her, trying not to appear nervous.

"What are you looking for, soldier?" The Lieutenant noticed her turn for the third time.

She thought quickly, "Union, sir."

"Good work, man." He then addressed the rest of his Company. "You all learn a lesson from Cotton! Keep watch! We're headed northward! Keep watch!"

Over the next hour or two, Della tried not to look back. She focused, instead, on her other surroundings, not the terrible man behind her. The smell of honeysuckle filled the air and drew her eyes up and outward. Breathtaking was the Shenandoah Valley. Wherever one looked, there were mountains. Delicate white blooms appeared randomly in the trees and yellow forsythia and pale mountain laurel painted the canvas of the wooded areas.

Della's eyes locked on a patch of blooming redbuds. A blue jay perched atop one. Its tiny claws wrapped around the twig on which it stood, and it fussed with something. Listening closely, she thought she could hear the *peep, peep, peep* of its offspring. It was a sound she had heard many times in Boone. Her mind wandered, entertaining images of a life gone by.

"Zebediah, don't you think about joining any army,"

Della instructed.

"I ain't *thinking* about it," he answered.

She knew what he meant. "What do you mean by that?"

"I'm done thinking, Dell. I'm doing it."

"I won't let you get yourself killed, Zeb. And Momma won't have it either."

"The Lord decides if a man lives or dies. You don't." he retorted.

Now for her brother, Della herself donned Confederate uniform and marched toward enemy territory. She thought about Zeb. And she thought about Josiah. Voices knocked her out of her funk.

"What did I tell you about keeping watch, men?!" called the Lieutenant. In a horny tone he said, "seek and ye shall find."

One soldier shouted, "That's a sight for sore eyes."

All heads turned in the same direction. Two young women on horseback trotted closer. The one in front flew a makeshift Confederate flag which romantically blew in the breeze. Its bearer bounced up and down, exciting every man present.

"Maybe they got something for us!" said one young soldier.

Burdock grunted in reply, "Something indeed."

When the females got close enough, the Lieutenant greeted them. "Mornin' ladies."

49

For the soldiers, it was a slowed down vision of two angels who had surely come to offer their sweet company and more. One was a dark-haired beauty. A true lady, she rode side-saddle to maintain her modesty in the presence of so many men. Light-haired and younger, the other rode up seconds later. While the dark-haired one conversed with the Lieutenant, the other untied a large satchel from the horn of her saddle. She sat on her leather perch, making eyes at the men below. A few of them thought they had peed their britches.

Della watched. The young lady made eye contact with her and smiled flirtatiously. Embarrassed, Della looked away. Feeling rejected, the girl looked away too.

"We're very obliged Ma'am. Thank you," the Lieutenant said respectfully. He took the satchel from the angel and nodded.

In unison, they pulled on the reigns and turned their horses away. The younger one looked back and blew a kiss. Hoots and hollers that sounded a little like a rebel yell echoed over them as the females rammed their heels hard into their horses and took off. A few of the men watched the women ride away. Many turned their attention to the Lieutenant who was thrusting his hand into the satchel and tossing out biscuits to his hungry soldiers. A couple of times, he helped himself to a bite before throwing. But no one seemed to care. To have the sight of good looking women and the feel of a satisfied belly at the same time was a thrilling combination.

"This biscuit's hard," one man said to another.

Smiling, the other replied, "I don't give a rat's ass!"

Two shots, like a double-tap, sounded over the celebration. Della dove to the ground. There was no cover. No trees. Nothing. All got low. A few just cowered, and those who had rifles returned fire. A minute or so later, the volley had ended.

"Cotton! Cotton!" John ran to his friend, frantic. He hadn't breathed this hard since Chancellorsville.

Slowly, the men rose, surveying the area for casualties and snipers. Whatever devil had taken those shots was gone.

Cotton replied, "I…I'm fine, John."

For fear of looking like a sissy, John did not hug his friend. But he felt a strange urge to.

As the confusion settled, word spread through the regiment that two were down. The Lieutenant lay twisted on his side, the saddlebag still in his grasp. His eyes half-open, he had no life in him. They moved him aside so he wouldn't be disrespectfully stepped over or on. They removed a prayer book and watch from his coat pocket. Burdock took the satchel (which had a few morsels left inside). The bedroll, canteen, and rifle were collected to use again. And his body was left there with one other dead man to keep him company.

Burdock savored the stale food. "Bitches." He looked at the Lieutenant one last time. "You have a good day, Lieutenant."

Chapter Seven

A few hundred canvas tents dripped soaking wet under the gray Confederate sky. Southerners and Northerners alike crouched inside, thankful that it was spring and not winter. On such a day, the number of sentinels was increased. It was known that Union devils were opportunists. And it could be counted on that, in the distraction of the unkind weather, there would be more escape attempts.

Josiah Jackson stood unshielded from the falling rain. Sogginess replaced the usual scratchiness of his uniform. His rifle a constant companion. At the start of each watch, the guard was read the Rules of the Confederacy pertaining to Prison Camps. Weapons must never be lain down except when hung on a rack away from the presence of prisoners. And there was no such place here. The prisoners were always present, and Josiah had yet to see any rack.

So he kept his rifle close at Belle Isle Prison Camp.

Situated west of the Confederate Capitol, it was far downstream from the natural shot tower at the stone bridge. Like the camp far up river, one would find no permanent buildings there. Tents as far as the eye could see. Then the deadly current of the James on both sides. The watery location deterred escape. For most.

Some days, when the good will of the sentinel coincided with God's gift of good weather, prisoners were permitted to swim in the river. Those healthy enough did so. And there had been the unfortunate few who were swept away, their slight bodies--thin from starvation and sickness--too weak to resist the current. It was sometimes thought to be a purposeful act, being drawn down into the soft water. Away from the southern hell of Belle Isle. Away from the hell of the war. It had been rumored that some of them bid onlookers goodbye before taking their final dip.

Then there were those who clung dearly to what remained of their lives. Surviving on tiny amounts of sustenance, all destined to become skeletal. It is shocking how bony a man can become and still be called alive. For many a stick man could be seen, still upright, and dreaming of the day when he might go home. Here among the starving, the rain poured down on Josiah Jackson. And all around him, Union prisoners crouched in dampness and boredom.

It was to Josiah's irritation that the Union allowed Negroes to carry weapons, to be called *soldiers*. And it gave him great satisfaction to know that many were returned to their proper confinement by the Confederacy. His preference would be that they be shackled, but he was pleased enough that the blacks at Belle Isle were no longer free.

He paced the perimeter of his assigned area. Alert in the rain, he kept watch for any movement. Union could not be trusted nor their slyness underestimated--black *or* white.

Under a nearby tent: "I'm gon do it. I caint take dis no mo. I'm doin' it."

His companion listened and said nothing.

The man continued. "I got nuffin to lose. I scaped once. I can scape twice." He looked at his companion hopefully. "You comin?"

His friend shook his head, eyes wide with panic.

"Den I'm gone." He darted out of the tent and into the soaking gray confusion. He had plotted his escape for weeks, and he could have run the route with his eyes closed. But he kept them open, nervously peering around as he hunched and ran through the noise and the raindrops.

Rifle in hand, Josiah was alerted by the sound of muddy sloshing and plodding. And he turned in time to see the dark soldier twenty paces away, moving swiftly toward the water.

The Rules of the Confederacy were explicit in the handling of escape attempts. Knowing he was justified, Josiah raised his rifle, took aim, and fired. The man went down, wriggling in the mud like a large worm. *He ain't going nowhere,* Josiah thought. He strutted toward his victim.

"Where you going, black man?"

Crestfallen was the man. His escape had been thwarted. But he felt a certain relief. For, the sentinel had shot him in the leg and not in the middle. *He stopped me but he don't wanna kill me.* He was relieved that he still felt his heart beating. Perhaps he would be sent to a hospital, be treated with some dignity. Perhaps a pretty nurse would care for him.

Josiah demanded again, "I said, *where* you going, black man?"

"I...I was goin' to take a pee in da riva, sah."

"Oh, was you?"

The man replied, "Yessa."

"I drink from that river, black man."

He nervously answered, "Yessa." His heart thumped a little faster. He had been called that name many times, but there was particular hatred in the voice saying it now.

The encounter gave Jackson a thrill. It broke the boredom. So he continued. For there were no superiors nearby to stop him. Both he and the man on the ground were aware of this fact.

"You think yer gonna make me drink your nasty rancid piss, black man?" He raised the muzzle and pointed.

All of the muscles in the man's face went numb and,

expressionless, he looked at his interrogator. "No." He thought that he might be speaking his final words, so he spoke them with conviction. "No sah, I wouldn't..."

A bang echoed through the rain and ended the conversation. Jackson stood, making certain that there was no further movement. With his boot, he touched one of the dead legs and nudged the lifeless man. He rubbed his own scruffy chin with his index finger. A few dozen eyes peered into the rain, looking for the one who shot and the one upon whom he fired.

From experience, Jackson knew to wait there. Within a minute or two, another sentinel or superior would arrive to take a report of what transpired.

"Another one of those sons a bitches tried to scape," he said to the approaching guard.

Among them all, it was known that Josiah Jackson was trigger happy. There had even been a time or two that he was questioned about his treatment of the prisoners. The sentinel looked at him. He knew that another man might have left this escapee alive. But he had enough work, and he wasn't about to create a stir over a black man who was, after all, a mere piece of property in the eyes of the Confederacy.

On Belle Isle, small crowds gathered when there was excitement. But today the bad weather kept would-be onlookers in their tents. And there were no prisoners close by who could dig a hole. So they bent down toward the dead man.

"Help me get him to the river," the other said. He put his hands under the man's large and powerless shoulders.

Careful not to touch the body with his hands, Josiah grabbed the cloth of the man's britches and dragged. Muddy, he finally made it to the river. Now free to go, they put him in and he was gone.

Chapter Eight

The Mennonite people of Harrisonburg moved freely about the camp. Their religious beliefs made them disagreeable with fighting, and the Confederacy declared them exempt from serving in the military. Life was peaceful and plentiful there. And these gentle people kept many a soldier fed during the war. There on the outskirts of town, the sight of seemingly normal life calmed the soldiers. It had been too long since they had seen any semblance of normality.

Della blended, disappearing into the crowd of men and boys. It felt less awkward now, to be among them, to be among none like herself. But there was a void in the absence of any womenfolk. And she longed for the kindness that men did not understand. For although she was used to them, she lamented the level on which they related. She wished to discuss more than killing yankees, lusty urges, and farts. Surely the more important men conversed about things more lofty, she thought. But her company was limited to the lesser figures, and her ears were limited to the common ramblings that went with them.

The homes in the Mennonite village stood out against the confusion of war life. The soldiers gazed as if it were a life-sized painting of Utopia. Green landscape undulated below rows of houses all different in color. All else seemed perfectly predictable. *Not like Boone,* Della thought to herself. Her eyes honed in on a bright red house. In front, a lady in a black frock and white bonnet draped pieces of cloth over a line while a little girl scurried between the flapping linens. She paid the impish child no mind, but kept about her business, turning once or twice to observe the new arrivals. A man with a wide-brimmed hat appeared in the doorway and motioned to her. She nodded toward him and continued her work. Standing there, he watched the gray procession moving closer.

The Lieutenant now gone, the cohesiveness of his small Company had dissolved and his men dispersed themselves among the others. Della made her way closer to John. He acknowledged his friend and nodded.

"What happened to your face?" Della inquired.

He scratched and shrugged in reply. A tomato-red patch lay across his forehead and cheek.

"You alright, John?"

"Damn muskeetos! I didn't see none anywhere. Did you?"

Examining his face, she carefully moved his hair aside with her hand. "No. I didn't see any." She smacked his hand away. "Don't scratch. It'll just get worse." She noticed splotches on his neck, but didn't bring them to his attention.

"This itches terrible, Zeb."

She pulled his busy arms down to his sides, saying, "Please *try* not too scratch. We'll find you some mud soon."

Thin and tired, the long line of men meandered over a swelling in the earth. From the sky, they looked like ants marching toward a crumb. And crumbs would have been very pleasing to them.

The camp was only visible from the crest of the hill, strategically shielding it from view. Descending, most breathed a sigh of relief. Camp meant rest and food. And it seemed that they were in the company of a hospitable people.

Now the monotony of the march would end. And soon a new monotony would begin. Men spread out and claimed spaces around the tents that were already there. Heavy packs and bedrolls were plunked down, relieving aching backs. It was a welcome confusion to most.

Cotton and Cumfrey stuck together. Nearby, three men worked together. "You boys lend a hand here!" one called to them. He handed them each two short rusted stakes. "Hold these. An, keep yer hands down."

Each steadied a tent stake to the ground while a man

pounded it down with a mallet. John remained still, resisting the urge to scratch his face.

In a fatherly tone, one of the men asked, "What happened to your face, boy?"

"Don't know. Probally bugs."

The man looked at him more closely. "Looks like ivy or sumac. You best get sumthin on that er it'll spread." His brows furrowed with concern. "An don't scratch if you kin help it."

"Yessir," he replied quietly, sheepishly glancing at Cotton.

For the next hour or so, the two worked their way around. Their smaller hands were perfect for steadying the little stakes, and they happily offered their specialized assistance while the larger men did the muscle work, careful not to hit the childlike hands of their helpers. When the work was done, they rested and hoped for a spot inside one of the tents at nightfall. The hard work created enough of a distraction that John forgot to scratch for part of the time. His face was now a light pink, but the skin around his eyes swelled.

Though young, they were exhausted and could think of no better thing to do than to sit. They sat together watching the activity all around the camp. Every few minutes, John lifted his hand to his face, sneaking in a scratch for which his friend would not chide him.

A short distance away, a Mennonite lady walked among

the soldiers in the camp. They did not notice from where she arrived. She just appeared. They watched her gentleness and grace as she floated from person to person doing God-knows-what. "What do you suppose she's doing?" Cotton asked John.

"Don't know." Uncomfortable, John had nothing jovial to say. And this disappointed Della who had grown used to his quips.

The woman meandered. From far away, they couldn't see her face, but they could see the form of her body. Her black dress hid her legs giving her the appearance of an angel gliding about. They watched her, mystified. Like a bee stopping at every flower, she skipped over none. And to each she offered a delicate nod. Her graceful hand lay on tired shoulders. To Della, the sight was striking; something so heavenly touching something so dirty and careworn. The lady was lovely, a lovely sight to behold.

John nudged his friend with an elbow. "Look." He pointed away from the lady. Throughout the camp, many Mennonite people walked among the hungry men, like missionaries in a foreign and Godless land.

Della was comforted by their presence. All of them moved about like angels. Her brain momentarily disconnected from her eyes and, in that moment, heaven was before her. Angels flitted about. She was among them yet removed from them in some way. Gossamer gowns blew gently in the supernal breeze. A tremendous light reflected off of every surface. She believed that it was God Himself. Her breathing slowed and feelings of warmth and safety overcame her.

And it was then that a figure appeared. Not an angel, but exuding a heavenly peace. He turned and faced her. Without moving, he beckoned. And she drifted effortlessly to him. *I haven't seen you in so long.* Her heart beat faster and her breath quickened.

She sat beside him. Taking her hand, he held it and put his other arm around her shoulder. And she let her head fall onto him. Relaxed, she was free from the fighting. In the presence of love. No heartbeat. No breathing. Only silence, brilliant light, and warmth. It seemed odd not being alarmed by the strangeness of it all.

"We'll meet again," he said to her.

Being pulled backward, she floated away from him. "I love you. Don't go." She lifted her arms to him and drifted away. "No!" Louder and with more passion, she yelled, "I'm sorry! Zeb! Zebediah!!"

A real hand touched her face. "Is that your name? Zebediah?"

Stunned, she didn't answer, but tried to process the unknown face in front of her.

"I'm Twila. I brought water." She held a small tin cup to Della's face.

Still confused, Della reluctantly took the cup and sipped. "Yes. I'm Zebediah Cotton."

"Where do you call home Zebediah Cotton?" She was taken by his features. She had never seen a boy with a pretty face before.

"Boone, North Carolina."

"Well, this is Harrisonburg, Virginia." She continued. "Do you mind if we pray?" She laid her hand on Della's shoulder.

"Please," Della replied.

Twila smiled approvingly and began. "Lord, I stand before You with your child Zebediah. I pray that you protect him. I pray that he be used to bring others to you, Lord. I pray that Your Will be done in his life. And I pray for those who love Zebediah, and who are missing him now. In Your Holy Name. Amen."

Della's lower jaw quivered and her eyes blurred with tears. "Amen," she agreed. She looked at Twila. "Thank you."

Motioning toward the red splotches on John's face, Twila commented, "Mother makes a good ointment for that."

Now reminded of it, John reached up and gave a healthy scratch. In unison, Della and Twila reached for his hand and pulled down. Two high-pitched voices ordered, "Don't scratch!" They looked at one another grinning. It was nice to be in the presence of another girl. Della felt less alone.

Looking at John, Twila said, "You look like you could use some prayer. What's your name?"

"No thank you," he replied shyly. He couldn't recall anyone having ever prayed for him, and it seemed an awkward thing.

"I've met a few named *No Thank You*." Laying her hand on his shoulder, she prayed without his permission. "Lord, bless this boy who won't tell me his name, the one with the itchy face. I ask that You protect him and heal him. I ask that he learn to turn to You for help. Amen."

John said nothing, but half-grinned and nodded at her. Around girls he was shy. He chewed his lower lip and looked away into the hillside, almost cowering.

"Your friend's a little shy," Twila said to Cotton.

"Yes. I guess because you're a girl." It crossed her mind that she, too, was a girl.

Twila looked at John, "If you'll come with me, I'll get that rash dressed." She turned to Cotton. "Zebediah, maybe you should come along. He might feel better if he's not alone with a scary *girl*."

"I'm not scared a you," John told her softly. "I just han't been around a lady in a while." He was careful not to say *ain't*.

Twila said, "I'm no one special sir. Just a servant of the Lord, trying to do some good to people. Now what's your name?"

"I'm John Cumfrey."

"John, I can help you if you'll let me." She nodded at them and walked up the hillside.

Behind her back, John nodded at Cotton with wide eyes, nervously gesturing for him to come along. The three walked up the hill in triangle formation: Twila leading, and Cotton and John together in the back. They walked along a row of houses. In some of the yards, women worked and offered friendly nods as Twila and her companions passed.

John looked at Cotton and mouthed quietly, "Must be Quakers." His face turned even redder when Twila heard him and turned around.

"We're Mennonite."

"Sorry," he replied.

Twila resumed a forward gaze and continued walking. "No need for sorrow." She led them into a brown house. It was distinguished only by its color. "Wait." She disappeared through a doorway and returned with a lady.

The two guests nodded at her.

"Good day, Ma'am," John said, trying to show manners. Twila was a pretty girl. And he couldn't remember the last time a pretty girl was sweet to him.

The lady came close. Careful not to touch, she cocked her head and honed in on his face. "Does it itch, son?"

"Yes, Ma'am."

She disappeared and returned with a tiny vessel. She swirled a small piece of cloth inside it for a few seconds, then touched the boy's face. Beginning at his nose, she stroked backward toward his ears and hairline. John stayed obediently still as she worked. The coolness felt good, and he could already feel the itchiness leaving. In a few minutes, she was done.

"There, son," she instructed, "You come back every day until that's gone."

"Yes, Ma'am," he replied. "Thank you, Ma'am." He looked at the pretty girl. "Thank you, Miss."

Twila smiled.

Chapter Nine

Days passed and John's face settled. "It feels much better," he said to Cotton, "but I think I'll git more salve put on it. For good measure."

"Your face looks fine," Della told him.

The redness was gone, but John reached up and scratched, "I can still feel a bit of an itch."

Della mocked him. "Bit of an itch."

"Are you mad at me, Zeb?"

"No." She tried to stop herself, but couldn't, "I don't see why you insist on going up there everyday. That dumb itch has *got* to be gone by now."

Frustrated, John retorted, "Well, what do you care if I itch or not?"

"I *don't*" snapped Della. "Just go. Go see Twila. Tell her *Good Morning* for me."

"I'll do that." He rose and stomped away.

She watched him walk up the hillside, noticing things about him that she hadn't noticed before. Whether she was angry at herself or at him she did not know, but she held her chin low and her brow furrowed as she glared. "Ignorant boy," she said to herself. And she kept her eyes on him, for the first time taking in the long legs and the way he moved on them. A kind of nausea overcame her as she watched him disappear.

"Mad at yer friend?" A voice snapped her out of her funk.

In no mood for idiots, she looked at Diggs and said, "What's it to you?"

He took one step backward, put his hands up, and spoke. "Easy, boy. Jus' making conversation witcha."

Della replied, "I'm not in a mood for conversation."

"By the way you were glaring, I would say he has sumthin to do with it."

She snapped, "Shut up!" Quietly she added, "He's the last thing I want to talk about."

Diggs smiled slyly. "Well, when you *do* feel like talkin bout him, you come see me and Henry. We been doin' some talkin' bout him too." He tipped his hat and walked away.

She looked up the hill, in the direction where John disappeared. She watched for him. But he was gone.

On the hill, Twila watched out the window. Like clockwork, John had come every morning. And she fully expected to see him. Trying to conceal her excitement, she called, "Mother. The soldier boy is here." Her face was reticent but her heart pounded. She opened the door before he had the chance to knock.

"Good Morning, Miss Twila," he said.

"Morning, John."

He removed his hat and tucked it under his arm. "Your salve is curing my itch."

"Good," she said. She searched his face, hoping for a lingering sign of redness. "You might should come back in the morrow."

His heart pumped a little faster, and a lump formed in the back of his throat. Unaware of the smile on his face, he replied, "if you think I should."

"I do," she replied.

"Good Morning, boy." Twila's mother entered with her ointment in hand. Examining the progress on the boy's face, she said, "You should be fine after today."

His heart dropped and disappointment shown upon his face as the lady stroked backward, applying the sticky covering. He had already come more times than were necessary, and he didn't want to push his luck. "Yes, Ma'am. I'm grateful for your care."

"Thank the Lord, young man. It is His work I do," she told him.

"Yes, Ma'am," he concurred. Awkwardly, he did as he was instructed and said, "Thank you, Lord."

Twila smiled approvingly.

"Daughter, fetch this young man a corn cake for his stomach."

She obeyed her mother and returned with a little parcel wrapped lovingly in a piece of cloth. "Here, John."

"Thank you, Miss Twila." He looked at her mother. "Thank you, Ma'am."

Twila smiled and her mother nodded. John walked out the door, already contemplating his next encounter with the pretty young girl. Twila entertained ideas of how to see him again without the appearance of impropriety.

"Come away from the window, daughter. There's a chicken that needs plucked."

Staring up the hill, Della saw the vernal masculine form descending toward her. He seemed more erect than before. A little more confidence in his stride.

When he was close enough to see the expression on his face, she became upset. She knew the look. It was a look she had seen countless times on Josiah Jackson. She approached him, wanting to interrupt whatever images were going on in his head.

"Well. Are you done now?" she asked.

"Done with what?" he inquired.

She wanted to say *Twila,* but she kept her composure. "You know…the poison ivy" She paused. "The ointment."

"I guess." Grinning, he added. "If I could see that girl every day, I'd march straight through another patch of poison."

"Mmmm," Della acknowledged him without offering encouragement or approval. She noticed the small cloth in his hand. "What's that?"

"Corn cake. From Miss Twila." he held it out to her. "Want some?"

She motioned it away. "No."

Unwrapping it, he began to eat. "Suit yerself." He continued, spitting crumbs with every few words. "Zeb, you know what it's like to be in love?" He was oblivious to her jealousy.

Cotton looked at the ground. "Yes, I know that feeling."

"You had somebody back home?" he asked his friend.

Cotton replied, "I did once." She paused. "But I don't anymore. I don't have anybody anymore."

John never heard his friend quite so down before, and he struggled to be encouraging. "You have me, Zeb."

For the first time, Della felt the magnitude of the lie. She thought, *if you only knew.* "No. You don't know me, John. You *think* you know me, but you don't."

"I know all the important stuff. I know yer the brother I never had." Not just saying them to comfort his friend, he meant these words. He meant them more than anything else he could remember saying.

Bitterness and irony plagued her spirit. But she replied, "Thank you."

Chapter Ten

From behind some brush, Burdock watched Della peeing in the woods. When the trickling stopped, he showed himself. "You don't do it like the rest of us, do ya?"

Horrified, Della looked up and fumbled to pull up her britches and rise from a squat position in one motion. She was too afraid to speak.

He grabbed her hands and held them to her sides. "Maybe you shouldn't pull those up just yet."

In her normal world, she would scream for help. But this was not the normal world. And a scream would expose her lie. So she tried to fight him off. In vain, her small frame wriggled under the strength of his 150 lbs. He clawed her harder.

Close to him, she could taste his breath, reeking with trench mouth. She avoided eye contact and fixed on his hairy, dirty face. He squeezed and panted, squeezed and panted.

He breathed stinking amorous threats. "It'll be more fun

for the both of us if you'd stop fightin me." He shook her violently, "Relax girl!"

Life had sometimes been rough and Della was no stranger to violence. God knows she had taken many a beating from her own mother. But to be taken by a filthy man this way. She had experienced nothing this grotesque, nothing this horrifying. Only the killing of her brother could compare. As he groped her and pressed himself into her, she told herself, *I lived through that, and I will live through this. Lord, I lived through that, and I will surely live through this.*

He raped her until he was done. She could feel it when he finished, and her whole body recoiled at the thought of his living seed continuing the assault. It would be easier to be shot. Yes, a bullet would be less an affront. *Lord, don't let his seed grow inside my womb,* she prayed.

As he dismounted her, she lost herself in the sky above. Fittingly dark. No stars to be seen. Just dark blueness over everything. She looked up and forgot about him for a few moments. In a deranged happy tone he told her, "Thank you. Much obliged…whatever your name is."

At that moment, she thought of killing him. If she could kill one bad man, why not two? What was the difference between Josiah Jackson and this man? Josiah had stolen something precious from Zeb. And now Burdock had stolen something precious from her. *I'm lying here unclothed* she thought. *And Zebediah is lying in the ground. Because of bad men. Because of bad men.*

Exposed, she lay there thinking about how such men took something that was meant to be beautiful. They took something meant to be good, and they mangled it and ruined it. Something needed to be done about them.

She stood and pulled her britches back on. They were wet, but she was not sure if it was from him or if she had peed when the monster surprised her. She gagged a little as she cinched them around her little waist. Then she sat and remembered a day some time ago. The last day she saw her brother, Zebediah.

It was different then. The Cotton family was whole. Even if Momma had a temper, they all knew they were loved. And there was hope for the future. Most of the folks in Boone lived as if there were no war at all. No one there owned any slaves. Isolated in their own little bubble, life went on as usual while the war raged in other places.

But even in lovely, quiet Boone, people did bad things. And one such bad thing happened to Zebediah Cotton one day. And it had nothing to do with Abraham Lincoln or Jefferson Davis, the Union or the Confederacy. In flowery, cottony Boone, something bad happened.

For at least a year, Della loved Josiah Jackson. Her heart felt the aches of young womanhood, and he became the object of her pangs. She longed to be near him always. He gave her new and different feelings even when she was only thinking of him. The excitement of it. Who would have imagined that a boy so handsome could love her?

In him, all of her questions had answers. She imagined a long life with him. Soon Josiah would propose marriage, and the idyllic rest-of-her-life would begin. That's what happens in life-- she believed. Now, Josiah never actually *told* her these things, but what does every young lady believe when being wooed? Besides, who would give such a costly piece of jewelry to someone unless they had intentions of marriage?

It was on a sunny day that Josiah presented Della with the beautiful locket. He knew what it would mean to her. She would know that he was serious. Determined to get what he wanted before he went off to fight, he wasn't about to let a good opportunity pass him by. And it was this very credo that had gotten him the locket as it sat unguarded in a little box in Old Lady Anderson's house. Josiah had grown accustomed to taking things without permission. And he would not, could not, return what he took. But before this day he had never taken a life.

Josiah and Della agreed to meet at the usual place in the woods. The place was Josiah's idea. There was a dead log that made a good bench for two people to sit on together. It was the same log that Josiah often used for target practice, standing rusted cans on it then picking them off one by one. An old shotgun he kept under some leaves and sticks beside the lady-entertaining log. So he would go there for whatever kind of excitement he could get. Girls or guns. Either would do. But he knew that he would get his fill of guns once he joined the Confederacy. So his main goal was to have the girl before he left. Della was his best bet. She was naïve, definitely not used up like some of the other girls who kept company with him. So between the three or four girls he had to choose from, Della was the one. She was the one whose acquiescence would be the biggest prize. So he hung the locket around her neck and kissed her softly.

The young pair cuddled and giggled as they perched on the log. Della's mind entertained images of marriage and children while Josiah's mind played images of a different sort. But all seemed to be going smoothly. Until Josiah knelt down before her. He got down on one knee, the way men do when they are about to propose. It was all utterly romantic to Della, and she was blind to his real intentions.

Zeb, however, was not. And he had seen all he needed to see. Wielding a stone the size of an apple, he yelled out, "You best get the hell off my sister, Jackson!"

Della screamed back at him, "Zeb! What are you doing?!"

He let the rock fly, hitting Josiah in the shoulder.

She ran to Zebediah. Grabbing at his swinging arms, she

screamed, "Zeb, stop! Stop it!"

"He's got no business touching you like that Dell!" She saw the anger in his face as he tried to reason with her. "What's wrong with you, girl?!"

"You're not my daddy, Zeb!"

He grabbed her arm and chided her. "You're coming home." She resisted and he yanked, "Come on!"

"Let go! You let go of me now!"

Josiah grabbed Della from behind and threw her to the ground. Shocked, she turned to see him, the love of her life.

"Josiah?" She paused in disbelief. When she saw the look on his face, her voice became louder. "Josiah!"

He fixed his gun on Zebediah. The lousy piss ant had foiled his girly entertainment. And now he would *be* the entertainment. Jackson pulled the trigger on his foe. *Bang!* Without pomp and circumstance, Zeb went down in a spray of buckshot.

Della crouched down by his body. Dangling around her neck, the shimmering token from Josiah gently skimmed Zeb's dead skin. She cried and begged to God, unaware of what words were coming out of her mouth. She shook him and implored him to wake up. He just lay there. Dead. Gone. No movement. When she could cry no more--it might have been minutes or hours--she lifted her head and looked around. As she had now expected, Josiah was gone. Long gone. Both of them were long gone.

What a terrible irony. In this very day, she had felt more loved than ever before. Now utterly alone. Her two most important men gone in one fell swoop. She gripped the chain with both hands and pulled, cutting open the back of her neck. It ripped in two pieces which she squeezed in hatred. Her fingernails dug hard into her own hands. She hurled the torn necklace and locket into the dead leaves and began undressing her brother.

Chapter Eleven

There was a piece of bacon for everyone. Carrying good-smelling baskets, Mennonite people made their way through the crowds of waking soldiers. Each man was given one piece of bacon and a corn cake. Food was plentiful in the breadbasket of the Confederacy, and the people of God there were cheerful givers. Truly devout to the teachings of the Bible, they loved everyone--if not in their hearts, then in their actions.

And the love flowed easier with the soldiers of the south. For the Confederacy honored Mennonite religious convictions and did not require that they partake in the fighting. But Union soldiers marched into Harrisonburg considering it enemy territory. They faced no aggression from the local people. Village Elders met with Union Officers proclaiming their neutrality and aversion to violence. But many of the peaceful young men were killed anyway. So, the people of Harrisonburg exercised forgiveness. They overlooked the constant reminders of tombstones and the Lincoln Farmstead itself. But they were pleased when Stonewall drove the Union out of the valley.

Soldiers clustered in small groups. Chronic coughing could be heard among them, especially in the cool morning air. Some scratched patches of poison ivy. All were thin and careworn. So they happily accepted the hospitality of the kind local people who meandered about, once again offering gifts.

John reached into a basket and came out with a strip of crispy pork. It was in his belly before he even got his corn cake.

"Hungry?" Della asked in jest. She was surprised by her own strength, that she could make a small joke after what had happened the night before.

John didn't answer, but just licked his fingers and watched for the next basket. When it came, it arrived with a familiar face. He smiled. "Good Morning, Twila."

"Morning, John. Would you like a corn cake?" she asked.

He reached inside. "Thank you," he said with sincerity.

She inquired, "How is your face?"

"Ma'am, I don't know. Would you mind taking a look for me?" He had not itched in days, but he welcomed the idea of her sweet hands touching him.

She placed the basket onto the grass and closely examined his young masculine face. The middle finger of her right hand gently caressed his cheek. A spark of something like adrenaline shot right through him.

"Your face is perfect." She didn't just mean that the redness was gone. She meant more.

Looking down, he pursed his lips to conceal a smile. But Twila saw it.

And Della saw it. "Twila!" She called firmly, attempting to pry her attention off of him. "Thank you for the corn cakes." She reached into the basket then handed it back to its owner.

"You're welcome, Zebediah." She whispered to them both. "Take another."

Both happily did so, and Twila continued her zigzag mission. John chewed and watched her as her work took her in another direction.

Della took small bites of the bacon, wanting the flavor to last as long as possible. She nibbled on the corn cake. Done with his, John watched her taking her time.

Della's lower abdomen ached. It had started the night before, after Burdock violated her. But the tasty food, and the presence of her friend, helped her to block it out. Momma had given her a shot of moonshine for cramps one time. It would be nice to have some now, she thought.

"Men!" A voice of authority called. John and Della looked up to see someone they did not recognize, obviously an Officer. "Captain requests you report to the supply tent. Bring any army issue weapons."

John and Della looked at each other. As of yet, Della had

no weapon. John's had been seized after Chancellorsville. The six or seven in their group immediately rose and headed for the supply tent. Della shoved the rest of her breakfast into her mouth and swallowed without chewing.

A line of men formed outside the tent. Inside, perched on a wooden chair, a Corporal sat behind a small table assuming a magisterial pose. Every few minutes, he flinched when the chair unexpectedly rocked. It may have been the bumpy earth, or it may have been that the legs were uneven. But he appeared convulsive whenever it happened. And this provided mild entertainment for the men waiting in line.

Della and John spotted Burdock ahead of them. Close behind, Diggs and Henry made quiet jokes about their twitchy superior behind the desk. To them it was hilarious. Burdock noticed the small commotion behind him and joined in.

"Well, now I've seen it all!" Burdock guffawed. "The Confederacy has the infirm leading us!" He mocked, "reporting for service, Officer Spastic!" He clunked his boots together and saluted. The three laughed like a pack of hyenas.

Della stared at them, honing in on Burdock. Her lack of expression was a concern to John, used to a smile or scowl, depending on the situation. But he had never seen the disturbing blank focus that was now upon her face.

"They trouble me," John said quietly. He jutted out his chin and motioned in their direction.

"They *are* troubling individuals," she replied, still looking straight ahead. "I don't trust them." She remembered the threatening comments made by Diggs, or maybe Henry. She didn't know which was which, but their mean faces were burned into her cognition now--as was Burdock's. Beyond mean, his was downright evil, and the very thought of it conjured fright.

But she was determined not to be his victim. Never one to surrender to such temptations, her resistance to martyrdom was proportionate to the severity of the crimes against her. So, it was her natural inclination to grow leathery skin in hard times.

"Stay away from them," her motherly instinct warned him. "Those are dangerous people."

"Oh, don't worry about that. I don't care for them, and they don't care for me." He felt a little ashamed. They hated him because of his horrible mistake in Chancellorsville. And idiots or not, it was his own fault that they picked on him.

Numb, Della watched Burdock until he finished his business and was gone.

"Next," someone called out. The line moved quickly and, within minutes, it was Della's turn.

"Name." The Corporal called in an official tone.

Now accustomed to using her dead brother's name, she answered naturally. "Zebediah Thomas Cotton, Sir."

He lazily raised his head from his paperwork. "Army issued weapons?"

"None, Sir."

He dipped his pen into the inkwell and made an X in a box next to Zeb's name. He repeated to himself, "None, Sir." Looking up at Cotton, he instructed. "See the Corporal at your right." He spoke in a mundane tone, and Della was glad to get away from him. He called to his counterpart, "Cotton, Zebediah Thomas."

"You look like a sharp person." Wanting confirmation, the weapon man asked, "Are you a sharp person?"

"If by that you mean smart, yes. I'm a sharp person," she answered.

"Good." He went to a pile of rifles. They had all been recently gone through and none had any serious malfunctions. "Learn to be a sharp shooter then." He handed her a scratched up rifle. She held it in two hands, trying not to look as awkward as she felt. "This weapon is a M1841 Mississippi Rifle. Here are your musket balls. Here is your powder." And he handed her two small drawstring pokes.

Not sure if she was supposed to say *thank you*, she nodded and walked away. She had never held a rifle before. But whatever ineptitude she had was tempered with curiosity. More than that, the weapon gave her a feeling of power. She rubbed her thumb against the notches carved into the butt. She knew what they represented, and she was respectfully solemn as she touched them.

Chapter Twelve

It was Twila's turn to churn the butter. Mennonites were known for crafting clever devices like the one-handed butter churn. A mother could actually nurse her child in one hand while making delicious butter with the other. Nothing more than a barrel on saw horses, the Mennonites made it a beautiful contraption, and it was capable of producing twice the butter of a traditional churn in half the time.

Twila turned the crank with her right hand. When she became tired, she moved her chair and cranked with the left. In simple surroundings, doing mundane things, her thoughts were anything but simple or mundane.

She had been taught to love God first and foremost. And she did. She loved Him with all her heart. But she had unanswered questions. Taught to love her brethren, she often wondered why she had to be separated from so many of the people in the world. It was acceptable to serve them, but not to fellowship with them. She once collected enough confidence to ask why her people kept a distance from others. *We have been separated unto the Lord,* her mother told her. And she never brought it up again. She wondered if God could possibly want her to be so lonely.

After some time, the sloshing of the cream had subsided. She gave her arms a rest and stretched her back in an arch. She turned the little cover on the churn and stuck her hand inside. She tasted. Perfect.

"Vilet!" She called in a moderately loud voice. It was not Godly or lady-like to yell. "Vilet! The butter's ready!"

The little child entered the room. Only five, she was old enough to take on a few simple chores. And one of those assigned to her was to put the freshly churned butter into molds. Having almost nothing that anyone would term *fancy*, the little girl loved the special butter molds. And she found that, if she had behaved herself, her mother was quite nice in allowing her the use of all of the pretty ones shaped like hearts and cows.

"I'm coming," she said to her sister. She placed her hands on her hips, "You *don't* need to yell at me," she told her.

"Vilet," Twila chided.

Obediently, Vilet stopped her scolding and collected what she needed to do her work.

A tall bearded figure entered the room. Both girls rose at attention. "Hello, father," they said in unison.

"Girls," he acknowledged. He circled a table in the room, inspecting it, his daughters, and their work. "Quarreling is wasted time. I expect more from my girls."

"Yes, sir," they answered, looking down in shame.

"Get to it. There are chores to be done," he instructed, then left the room.

Looking down, they listened until they could no longer hear his footsteps. When all was clear, they looked at one another and giggled.

"Now you do your work, young lady," Twila mocked. She gave her little sister a mock swat on the bottom and went outside. The air was cool, and a soft breeze began to blow down from the mountains. She closed her eyes and let it caress her face.

When she opened her eyes, she fixed her gaze downward, down the hill toward the encampment. From where she stood, the men blended together in a smear of gray against the green grass. A sudden gust from the other direction blew her hair into her face, and a few little strands stuck to her eyeballs. She tucked them behind her ears, and into her bonnet. She pulled one tickly piece from her mouth and shook it to the ground.

It was then that she felt that eeriness that you get when someone is watching you. She felt it for certain. But she was uncertain who or where. Uncomfortable, but not afraid, she looked around. She saw no one. The closest people within view were the blur of men at the bottom of the hill. Maybe it was Vilet, or her father, or some other Mennonite. They did have a way of staring at people. She shrugged it off and went back inside to resume her chores.

Burdock watched her disappear. The events of the night before piqued his interest in amorous interactions. Oh, and that Twila was more comely than the soldier girl. What happened with Della. *That* was the act of a desperate man. *That* was an opportunity. A man has needs. Lady luck presented him with the opportunity to have his needs met, and he wasn't about to let that pass him by. But now he was reminded of how it felt to be with a woman. It had been too long, way too long for him. And his time with Della made it better, but somehow made it worse. Now his desire was inflamed. He was like a wild animal on the prowl, like a sniper taking aim. And Twila was in the crosshairs.

Chapter Thirteen

"What you wanna do is dump yer powder down the barrel. Put in yer ball. Ram it. Rock yer hammer back and hold on!" The soldier handed the rifle back to Cotton, adding, "It's gonna be smoky, so make sure there is something close by to give you cover after you shoot." He nodded his head goofily and smiled as Della took her weapon and walked away.

And that was the extent of her training with a rifle. Back in Boone, she could hit a small tree with a stone from twenty or thirty feet away. So she considered herself to have a good eye. The thought had never crossed her mind to aim at a living creature, but she was thinking differently now. And she had two specific targets in mind.

She would have liked to practice some, but ammunition was in low supply and could not be wasted. One less musket ball in battle could cost a soldier his or her life. So she took practice shots in her mind. On the left stood Josiah Jackson. On the right,

Burdock. They were close enough so that she could make out their ugly faces. Had they been farther, imagining the shot would have been difficult. But able to see who they were, the evil in them stood out. Obviously, these were targets deserving of the musket balls that would be fired at them. When the time came, she would be willing to spare a few.

Not too far away, she saw her friend John. Even in the small crowd, he stood out to her. Without thinking, she walked toward him. It was the natural place to go.

"John," she called.

There had been some hold up at the supply tent, and she had given up waiting for him.

"Look, John." She held out the rifle, like a child showing off an amazing Christmas gift.

Embarrassed, John tucked his new weapon, a knife, into the back of his belt. Seeing that he was empty-handed, she immediately toned down her enthusiasm.

John was pleased for his friend. "A rifle," he said, half a statement and half a question.

"I know," she answered.

John asked, "Do you know how to use it?"

"Of course I know how to use it," she stated, slightly insulted. "You put the powder and the ball in, ram it, and shoot."

"Uh-huh," he stated.

It seemed awkward to not ask, so she reluctantly

proceeded with the question. "Did you get one?"

Sheepishly, he replied, "No." Reaching back, he retrieved the blade and removed it from its scabbard. To be sure, he was not its first owner. But the blade was shiny, and the sun reflected off of it as he tilted it to show his friend. "I don't think they'll be givin' me any more guns." He looked down. "But they said that a man had a right to protect himself. So, this is my protection." He didn't intend to get close enough to any yankees to use it. "I guess they figure its harder to make a mistake with a knife and, from close up, even a fool like me would know if they was a yankee or a gentleman."

The thought crossed Della's mind that a man was not a *gentleman* just by virtue of not being a yankee. She could think of at least two southern men who were not.

"Don't worry, John," she assured him. "Between the two of us, we'll be fine."

She smiled at him, but he did not return the gesture. He just looked up the hill as if waiting for someone. The thought of Twila made him forget his failures. He didn't consider why. But it was because she saw no failure *in* him. What mattered in a man was not his station or popularity. To Twila, it was the heart. And in John, she identified a kind heart. So, while his spirit longed for the way she made him feel, his heart longed for her. And he watched up the hill for the girl to whom he was not an idiot.

She could hold back no longer. "Are you looking for Twila?" Her tone revealed the level of her emotion. "Because I really don't think I can stand anymore of your pining. We're in a war, John!"

"That ain't right, Cotton," he said to her.

"What *ain't right*," she mocked, "is a soldier thinking about a girl when he should be thinking about other things." What she felt was that he was thinking about the *wrong* girl.

"Exactly what *other things* do you want me to be thinking about?!" He threw his arms up in disgust. "I don't get you, Cotton." With that, he walked away. Of course, up the hill.

There were others close by, so she was careful not to look too upset. But, again, Della watched him walk away from her when all she wanted was for him to come toward her. *What did I just do?* she thought. She had made Zebediah disappear. And now she was making John disappear.

He reached the top of the hill, but could not bring himself to approach the house. What would he say? What reason would he give for being there? He couldn't pretend, anymore, that he still had poison ivy. He imagined that he possessed enough courage to get her and tell her his true feelings. But he did not.

He moved among the houses, staying on the main path so he wouldn't look conspicuous. Blowing off steam and walking off anxiety, he paced back and forth. Twila's house was the only brown one among them all. And looking around, John noticed that there were no two houses painted the same. The varying colors gave them the illusion of being different. But, for the first time, John saw that they were not different. In fact, they were all exactly alike. Upon inspection, it appeared that each and every one was made in the same way by the same maker. It dawned on him that the Mennonite people dressed alike, but that the women wore dresses of differing colors. It crossed his mind that they all had the same Creator. He wasn't sure if he believed that, but he knew by now that they did.

Tired, he found a place under an oak and sat, resting against its trunk. A few acorns poked his now-bony behind, and it hurt. But he really didn't care enough to get up and move them. He let his eyes fall upon the encampment where he saw gray blurs interrupted by a few campfires starting. Smoke drifted up, and he let his eyes follow it skyward.

"John Cumfrey," a soft voice said to him. He took it as his imagination and remained still. He turned his head when he felt a gentle touch on his arm. He came to a few seconds later, realizing that he had real company. And amazing miracle of miracles, the object of his desire.

From the window, Twila's father watched.

When John really wanted to say *sweet dear heart,* what came out of his mouth was, "What are you doing here?"

Twila would have preferred the former. "I live here, sir." She eyed him quizzically. "What's wrong?"

"Nothing's wrong," he replied, lying.

"Of course something is wrong. Now tell me what it is," she pressed him in her gentle way, seeing the redness in his eyes.

A second from telling her that he loved her, he stoically answered, "I guess I'm just tired."

She looked him in the face, listening attentively.

"I'm tired of this war. I'm tired of going from place to place all the time. I'm starving. Look at us. We're all starving." He meant what he was saying, but with every word he wished he was telling her something entirely different.

She took his hand in an act of compassion. Embracing it inside both of her warm hands, she brought it toward her and laid her face upon it. A rush of warmth swept over him. His face reddened and his pupils opened. Inside her hands, his paralyzed hand tingled, and he thought that he might pass out. But he didn't.

"Twila?" he softly whispered. When she raised her face, he touched it with his other hand. At that moment everything in the world was good. Nothing was amiss. He was touching her the way he wanted to. She was permitting it. He forgot the war. He forgot his own shortcomings. He forgot about Cotton.

"What is it, John?" she asked almost inaudibly.

"I...I..." He couldn't do it. "I want to thank you for all of your sweet kindness."

She smiled shyly as he spoke.

He continued. "I don't think such a pretty girl has ever been so sweet to me before." Though these were not the words he wanted to be speaking, he was sincere when he said them. "I...I..."

When she saw him getting flustered, she put her hand to his lips and said, "Shhh. I know. I care about you too, John."

He couldn't believe what he was hearing. Nothing in his life had ever gone the way he wanted it to. But now a beautiful angel sat beside him telling him that she cared. He thought he might be dreaming. But the breeze, her touch, and the smell of smoke told him that he was wide awake. Wide awake indeed.

Chapter Fourteen

Burdock never gave much thought to anything. The exception would be times when he was hatching some scheme to get something he wanted. Sometimes it was money, sometimes a woman, sometimes someone's pride. And in many cases, getting those things required no thought or planning at all. In fact, he was amazed at how easy some people made it for him. And he had a way of finding those people who did this exceptionally well.

What he wanted now would not be handed to him. Nor would it be very hard to take. He was a rough, hardened man. He knew how to be sly. He could cover his tracks, even make it look like it was someone else as he slipped away, blameless.

He sat near the campfire sharpening his blade, paying no mind to the ignoramuses around him. They were mindless animals. And he had no patience for them, or for anyone.

Unbeknownst to Twila, she was a popular young lady this

evening. She combed Vilet's hair in the candlelight, oblivious to the fact that several people were thinking of her. She would have been happy to know that one of them was John, the kind-hearted soldier boy. He sat opposite Cotton at the campfire, thinking only of his sweet Twila. Della watched him through the flames, knowing where his mind was. In vain she tried to block images of Twila and John sparking by the oak tree.

Twila's father lay in bed thinking about what he saw that evening. His sweet daughter showing interest in a boy, an *English* boy who was fighting in a war. For all they knew, he had killed. Wisdom told him that he should say nothing. For, the encounter looked innocent enough. And it was human nature to desire the forbidden. So he decided to leave the situation alone and trust that Twila would not stray from her upbringing. Yet, the wanting to collect his children and take them away to safety gnawed at him.

He would have been sick to know that a filthy man like Burdock was thinking of her too. Sitting in the dirt like a snake, back hunched and elbows pressed down on bent knees as he whittled the end of a stick into a point. He stopped and ran his thumb down the edge of his newly-sharpened knife, flinching when he felt a slice. Bringing his injured thumb to his eyes, he smiled and nodded. "Knife's good and sharp now. Good and sharp." Some of the men noticed, but they had learned to keep their distance, and they refused to interact with him.

He stared into the flames and laughed to himself, picturing Twila underneath him. The idea of her squirming and pleading excited him. He loved the feeling of power it gave him when a person, especially an innocent, was begging him for mercy. Again and again, he went to the same place in his mind, looking forward to the moment that it would become reality. He was the kind of evil that the Mennonites prayed against. And the prayers worked--most of the time.

When Vilet fell asleep, Twila opened her Bible. As far back as she could remember, it had been her custom to read from Scripture in the morning and at night. She liked to have God's Word be the first thing and the last thing fed to her spirit. Tonight she read from Luke.

And there will be signs in the sun, moon, and stars, and upon the earth distress of nations bewildered by the roaring of sea and waves: men fainting for fear and for expectation of the things that are coming upon the world; for the powers of heaven will be shaken. And then they will see the Son of Man coming upon a cloud with great power and majesty. But when these things begin to come to pass, look up, and lift up your heads, for your redemption is at hand.

She closed the book, kissed it and placed it on a small table next to her bed. Seeing her sister's beautiful little sleeping face, she blew out the last flame in the house and closed her eyes.

The Mennonite people were hard workers and, as a result,

they were good sleepers. Their Godly lives were so full, balanced, and devoid of all things unhealthy. In their waking hours, they strove to do everything as unto the Lord. And it only made sense to do so in their non-waking hours. Each night, Twila's father prayed for a good night's rest for his family. He prayed that they be refreshed in the morning, and be given whatever was necessary to do God's work in the next day. Since the war, he made it a point to say a special prayer for their safe keeping. And tonight was no exception.

When it got as dark as it could get, Burdock left the fire. Some of the men had gone to sleep, and the ones who were still awake were used to seeing him suddenly disappear. So it was no big matter when he left. Avoiding the path that most people took, he ascended the hillside keeping to the fringes. It didn't matter that it was too dark to see. It was his habit to be stealthy.

At the front door of the house, he took out his knife. Without making a sound, he slid the thin blade between the thick oak door and the jamb. Seeming to know the exact spot, he lifted until he felt the weight of the wooden bolt. Pushing it up, the door opened without so much as a squeak. And Burdock entered where he did not belong, knife in hand.

In another room, Vilet murmured in her sleep. "Don't run away, kitty cat." She rolled over, striking Twila in the face with her hand. Already headed in that direction, the female voice told the intruder that he was dead on.

The hit from her sister awoke Twila. And when Burdock entered the room, her pupils had opened just enough so that she could make out the male figure standing at her bedside. "Father?" she called quietly.

Now seeing as keenly as a creature of the night, Burdock cupped his whole hand over her mouth and nose and pressed down.

"You shut up. You shut up, or I'll kill her."

From the terror, and the pressure on her face, she felt that her eyes would explode. But they did not. And she held them wide open as he grabbed her and forced her out of her house.

She had never seen violence, and she was taught against it. So, she could think of nothing else to do but go with him. And if she stirred up his anger while still close to home, Vilet might pay the consequences. Terrified, she went with him into the night.

Having always remained inside the safe walls of her home after sunset, the darkness was a foreign thing to Twila. But the shadowy time was Burdock's natural surrounding, and it was there that he felt most at ease, able to do what he wanted to whom he wanted--and with the least resistance.

Is he going to kill me? she asked herself. She thought that she should pray in case she was about to go home to the Lord. She had tried to live a life that was pleasing to Him, but she thought it a wise thing to repent in such times. As he led her farther away from home, farther away from anyone's home, she began to pray. It was not a fearful prayer, but one of repentance and thanks and praise. Speaking ever so softly, she called out to her God. *"Father in heaven, I am sorry for my sins. I thank You for your sacrifice and for my salvation. In this hour, I praise You dear Lord."* She lifted her eyes to the night sky as if reaching.

"What in the hell are you doing, stupid girl?" Burdock said to her. For, it was not a question, but a statement of her foolishness.

She replied, *"For the doctrine of the cross is foolishness to those who perish, but to those who are saved, it is the power of God."*

His anger flared. But it was alright with him, because it would make it that much more satisfying when he took what he wanted from her. Grabbing the back of her night shirt, he forced her along, all the while keeping the cold metal blade ready. He took her over a knoll, knowing that it would absorb the sounds of any crying or screaming.

Fully cognizant of her own steps, she felt the earth beneath her feet, taking special note of exactly how it felt to be grounded there, how it felt to walk upright in this body. She was aware of the knife, having noticed it glistening in the small amount of moonlight. She considered that it might be inside her flesh this night. But she did not fear that outcome. The thought of it seemed more like the answer to a riddle than something to fear. For she had been taught that life is everlasting with God and she feared the loss of nothing on this earth, not even the breath in her own body. She knew that the most important thing could be taken by no human.

"Take that off!" he ordered her. He could have easily done what he wanted with her nightshirt on, but he enjoyed shaming people. And a young Mennonite would surely feel shame in her nakedness.

Her eyes had now adjusted very well to the darkness. And without having to think about it, she just stood there looking at her abductor.

"I *said* take that damn thing off!" It was like a fun game to him, the back and forth of the demands and the resistance. He was like a cat tossing a mouse into the air.

"I can't," was her answer.

"The hell you can't, slut! Take it off!" He was becoming annoyed. He should have been enjoying her by now.

Strangely calm, she told him, "No."

Oh no. I picked me a insane one, he thought. *She don't even feel fear!* "Don't you know what I'll do to you, bitch? Believe me, I kin get that frock off a you! I'll skin you alive if I want!"

In a conversational volume, she began to speak to God. *"Lord, this man means harm to me. If it be Your Will that my life be finished, please take me quickly."*

Seething, he threw her to the ground and put his heavy, smelly body on top of her. It felt good, but he grew more agitated as she continued.

He yelled at her. "You ain't gonna quit, are ya?"

She blocked him out and thought only of her God and her new love John. Oh how sorry she felt. Just budding, their love would be pruned off the bush never to bloom. How sorry she felt for him, having to go on without her while she lived in the eternal comfort of heaven.

"God, Bless John. Bless sweet John. Don't let him be lonely, Lord. Let him know You."

Burdock tore at her clothing, enraged now. He had finally gotten down to her nude form and he was about to take what he came to get. While she continued her prayers, oblivious to him, he rubbed up and down on her lower body like a dog, attempting to penetrate her. But the anxiety from her holiness rendered him unable, and in a frothing rage, he slit her throat. Dismounting, he pulled up his britches and spat at her. "You stupid bitch!" he said, and left her for dead.

With every heartbeat, blood spurted from her neck. This life was escaping from her and she was surprised by the lack of pain. Beginning to die, extreme tiredness was what she felt. The final strand holding her to this life was John. *I need to let him know that I love him.* She couldn't go without doing so. Using her last ounces of energy, she rolled over and, with a bloody hand, scratched his name into the dirt. He would know now. She could go. In her mind, she again asked God to take her quickly, and He did.

Chapter Fifteen

Just like on any other day, the sun rose in the morning. It rose on the just and on the unjust. But it was quieter than usual. No Mennonites wandered the encampment with baskets. The air was still, and it even seemed as if there might be no birds in the sky.

Della lay there looking up, trying to think of a reason to rise from her bedroll. Sitting up on one elbow and looking around, she saw that John was not there. Unable to think of one good reason to get up, she lay back down while those around her began to move about. Lazily watching the clouds pass in the sky, she noticed a vulture flying high above, beginning to circle. She watched his black wings, wide open against the light blue background. He glided through the blueness going around and around in a death dance.

On the hill, Twila's mother stood, chest heaving up and down with panic, heart pounding three times its normal rate. Her girl had never walked off before in the morning. Not without asking. Her head darted left and right. She turned her whole body about and repeated, searching east and west, hoping to see her daughter. Perhaps she went to the well. Perhaps to the privy. But the mother knew better. She knew Twila's habits. And disappearing was not one of them.

Hyperventilating, she started to run, not having any real destination in mind, just wherever Twila might be found. "Oh Lord." She breathed quick shallow breaths between phrases, and her eyes darted back and forth. "Lord, where's my girl? Where's my girl." Not knowing what else to do, she began pounding on the doors of the houses. And she didn't wait for anyone to answer, but instead went to the next door sobbing and calling out. "Help. Somebody help. Where's Twila? Where's my Twila?" Her motherly instinct drove her fear, telling her that something terrible had happened. And that instinct had never betrayed her before.

Soon she was joined by her husband and some of the other villagers. Vilet ran to her crying mother. "Mother! Mother, what's wrong?" She began to cry. "Where's Twila, Mother?" A young girl quietly took her by the shoulders, gently ushering her to another home, where the child could be shielded from whatever trial had descended upon them.

The men formed search groups. The women consoled the frightened mother and brought her away to another house where she would be offered tea and prayer.

Near the woods at the edge of the camp, John was busy throwing his newly-issued knife at a tree. He hit the tree every time but, half the time, the knife pinged against the bark and dropped to the ground. He had a lot to think about, and the repeated activity and the aloneness allowed him the environment in which to contemplate all that was going through his mind.

Still feeling something like elation, it was now tempered with anxiety over his argument with Cotton. He threw again and the blade stuck, making a quick vibrating sound before settling into stillness.

He remembered the day he and his friend waded in the James River collecting musket balls. He remembered the comfort it gave him to have a friend when so many others hated him. Cotton didn't judge. It seemed a cruel irony that, just as he had been given the love of an angel, his best friend should be taken away.

The commotion on the hill intensified, getting the attention of some of the waking soldiers. Before long, many men could be seen standing and pointing up the hill. One said, "Something's goin' on up there with those Mennonite people."

Della got up. Having not seen John today, her concern grew. She asked no one in particular, "What's happening?" It was obvious that there was a situation of some urgency. Even from the distance, you could see that villagers were gathering, and that some moved quickly about searching for something or someone. At that moment, John appeared, still playing with his knife. Covered in bits of bark and dirt, he cleaned it off on his shirt.

"John," Della said, relieved.

"Morning, Cotton," he offered, trying to decipher the tone of his friend's greeting.

Side-by-side, they faced the Mennonite village, taking in what information they could gather from the scene. Many soldiers thought it best to stay out of whatever was going on. Others made their way upward, toward the confusion.

As if struck by a bolt of lightning, John panicked, "Twila!" He ran up the hill, Della following behind him. She felt no jealousy, only concern for the kind girl. And concern for the boy, certain now, that she loved.

When they reached the place where the people were gathering, John pushed his way to the middle, searching each face. "Where is she? Where is she? What's going on?"

A lady in an orange dress took him aside. "Easy son."

"Who are they looking for?" he begged.

"Twila, son."

His heart sank. All his life, he had a way of spreading bad luck. And it was no surprise to him that something bad might have befallen her. The only thing he could think to do was run. Instinct, and the vultures circling above, told him where to go, and he bolted toward the knoll at the edge of the village.

Not very far away, Twila's bereaved father knelt beside her cold body, sobbing. "My beautiful child, Lord," he cried. "My precious child." Visceral sounds bellowed out of him, echoing past the knoll and into the town. Lovingly, he lifted her and began to carry her home.

Approaching the bloody scene, John saw them rounding the top of the small hill. Several townspeople surrounded their grieving brother, forming a hedge around him. Seeing John's grief, they allowed him in when he reached them.

"Please let me see her," he begged in between sobs, "Twila, oh Twila! I'm so sorry." He touched her cheek as he had the night before, but now it lacked any movement. He could not have been prepared for the feeling it gave him when she failed to respond and he was certain that he was losing his mind. "She's so beautiful." He looked at her father. "I'm sorry." Turning, he ran as fast and as far as he could.

Della ran behind him, "John! John!"

He cried harder than ever before. More than when Stonewall died. And the running was an automatic attempt at releasing the pressure inside him. He did not know how much time had passed when he stopped. And he did not know where he was.

Chapter Sixteen

In the afternoon, some of the ladies of the village walked to the spot where Twila crossed over. Their mission was to clean the area and restore it to it's original peacefulness. For they did not want Vilet or Twila's mother to happen upon anything that would cause distress. Indeed they did not even want them to know the spot where the brutality occurred.

They walked in respectful solemnity, looking much like they did the first day that they welcomed the newest batch of soldiers. Gracefully they floated across the ground, backs arched in lady-like curves, and chins pointed downward. But today they seemed to lack the joy that shown in them before.

One of the ladies carried a Bible and another carried a large basket. Yet another carried a bucket. When they came to the spot, they had a prayer before touching anything. They prayed that God would send his Holy Spirit to cleanse the area where such evil had been done. They prayed that the demons that drove someone to do such a dreadful thing be cast away into hell, never to return. And when they finished, they got about the business of removing the physical reminders of the event.

"Sister?" one called to another. "Look." She pointed to a message scratched into the soil. They bent down to take a closer look. "What do you suppose that says?"

They all gathered in unladylike squat positions, squinting and bending. One said, "I would say that it says *John.*" They looked at one another quizzically.

Several nodded in agreement. "I believe so, too," one said. But they knew of no one by that name in their village, and wondered what the cryptic message meant, and who had written it: Twila…or the person who killed her.

Not knowing what they would do with this information, they focused on the job at hand. In the bloody brown dirt, they found a small wooden cross. For a number of years, Twila carried it wherever she went. It could always be found with her…in a pocket, a basket, or in her hand.

One lady crouched and picked it up reverently, cupping it in two hands and placing it gently in the lined basket. Once inside she covered it so lovingly as if it were Twila herself. In a mini shroud of white cloth, it would be given back to the girl's mother and father.

There seemed to be no other personal objects. Only dried blood and the mysterious word on the ground remained. The ladies stood silently for a moment, bowing their heads in quiet prayer. For the blood of their fallen sister lay mingled with the dirt before them. And when they finished paying respect, a bucket of water was used to wash away what was left of her.

In the camp, there was news. News of the death and news that the entire Division would be on foot again within days. It was all bad, so bad to Della. John had not returned, and he was in no mind to be alone. She kept her focus on him and him alone. Having let herself think about Twila a couple of times, it nauseated her and pressed on her heart with the heaviest oppression. So, she kept her eyes off of the hill, but she looked everywhere else for her friend.

The brown house was full of Mennonite people offering comfort to the grief-stricken family. Twila's body lay on the table where she had dinner each night. Four women removed her torn bed shirt. A cloth was wrapped loosely around her neck, concealing the injury. They washed her body in warm water and covered her in perfume. They also washed her hair. Silken, it cascaded onto the table around her shoulders. The women took the utmost care in combing it, and tucking it under a clean new bonnet.

"Sister, I'll have the burial clothes now." She held out her hands and received a plain white gown. It was the same one that was used for all of the female innocents, the ones who had passed at an early age. "Please," she said, gesturing for some help.

One lady sat the little girl up while another raised her delicate arms, allowing the garment to be placed over her head. What a sad sight for the people there, and one they would never forget. But it was not the first nor the last time that they would perform this task. And it was custom that the mother of the deceased be spared. For it was too much for a mother to bear.

Removed from the area where her daughter was being prepared, Twila's mother sat in a rocking chair holding her Vilet in her lap. The bereaved child buried her face into her mother's bosom and nuzzled there, refusing to look at anyone. Her mother lovingly stroked her hair, giving her the surplus of love that Twila had left behind. A look of sad surrender covered the woman's face. She let the rocking comfort her, saying quiet prayers in her head.

Two ladies in black dresses gently approached her. They were some of those who had cleaned the spot over the knoll. Side-by-side, they knelt before her, touching her ever so gently on the hand and arm. The Holy Kiss was exchanged. "We are so sorry for you, Sister. We pray for your comfort."

"Thank you," she replied in a whisper. Her face remained expressionless, broken. She rocked as they touched her.

One of the ladies reached toward Vilet offering a caress. The child jerked away, making a *nya* sound. Under normal circumstances, a Mennonite child would be severely scolded for such disrespect toward an adult. But she was granted leniency considering her terrible loss.

"We have brought you something, Sister," one of them said. She held out her palm, presenting a small parcel in white linen. The mother took it and felt through the cloth. Recognizing the cross shape, she knew what it was, and she broke down, sobbing and squeezing Vilet tighter as she rocked.

"Please, Sister," one of them beckoned. "May we have another moment?"

Suppressing her tears as best she could, she gave them her attention.

"We found something else."

The mother searched their hands expecting another one of Twila's belongings. *What could it be?* she wondered. For the girl owned so little. Not even so much as a ring or locket. "What is it?" she asked.

With some hesitation, one of them answered. "Well, it's hard to say, Sister. We don't really know what to make of it." She paused. "But we believed it the right thing to tell you."

Anxious now, the mother sat more erect and waited for their reply. Vilet continued to burrow into her mother's chest.

"On the ground, Ma'am." It was hard for her to say, and she took frequent pauses as she spoke. "On the ground where it happened...we found something scratched into the earth."

Confused, Twila's mother listened carefully.

"Why…what…*what* did you find?" she pleaded softly.

"It was a word, Ma'am…It said *John*."

Dismayed, she recoiled in thought. "John."

Chapter Seventeen

Since May, General Lee had been steadily fortifying his troops around Culpeper. Happy to be out of the isolation of Belle-Isle, and happy to be away from the constant company of Union devils, Josiah welcomed the change. And his leaving pleased his superiors at the prison camp who were happy to be rid of the escalating concerns and questions surrounding him. So, they gave him his papers, money for a railroad ticket, and sent him on his way.

It was the first day in a very long time that the thought of Josiah Jackson did not cross Della's mind. First, the fight with John, then the unspeakable discoveries the next morning. There was enough turmoil in her immediate surroundings to consider without thinking about a cur like Jackson.

And then there was the question that no one had yet asked. What devil could have done this? It was a question that the Mennonite people would not consider until their lost child was properly laid to rest. But, now, it weighed heavily on Della's mind. When contemplating the crime, one name alone surfaced. Burdock. That filthy Burdock. Building on her knowledge of what he had done to her, she imagined that he did the same to poor Twila. And for reasons unknown, he ended it in taking the unfortunate girl's life.

Sitting in her usual place, surrounded by her few worldly possessions, Della stared toward the village. Soon, movement could be detected. And she was not the only one watching. Many eyes in the encampment had been anticipating the ensuing procession. Almost all of them had seen the blood of battle. For, many comrades and enemies had fallen before them. But this was different. Exceptionally sad. Exceptionally moving for all who witnessed it…all but one.

Absent were the joyful colors of the women. Dressed in the color of mourning, they moved slowly together like a dark cloud drifting across their town. Unheard by the watching soldiers, they prayed quietly as they walked. Even as their tears dropped to the ground, all remained respectfully upright. Before them, Twila lay. Two on each side, young men carried her in an unassuming box made for such an occasion. Moving slowly in unison, they impressed many of the soldiers.

A short distance from Della, Burdock stood and watched. "Terrible," he said in his gruff voice. That's all he said. Just *terrible*. But as he looked on, he entertained images of events with Twila. It was especially satisfying that she was the apparent sweetheart of that traitor boy. He saw it all as having fit together like a puzzle. That dumb girl. All she had to do was open her legs. If she had given him what he wanted, she'd be bringing him breakfast in the morning. And the fact that her death was particularly painful to John Cumfrey...*that* was a bonus! The little bastard might have cost the Confederacy the war!

Without song, they lowered her down in silence. Using her mother's dress, Vilet wiped her wet and boogery face. And holding one another tightly, wiping away their own tears, the grieved parents watched the box descend away, acutely aware that it housed the empty shell that was their first born.

An elder spoke. "Lord, this child was Yours in life, and we give her back to You now. May her soul be with You in Glory."

A number of soft *Amen*s were replied.

The pall bearers remained, and everyone else walked away, each person knowing his or her own assignment in consoling and caring for Twila's family. When the crowd had gotten sufficiently far from the grave, the remaining men shoveled dirt into the hole.

The smell of apple pie wafted through the brown house. Hours before, some of the ladies set about baking comforting foods for the bereaved and their visitors. But Twila's family would not be eating that day. Her mother resumed her post in the rocking chair, consoling her own broken heart with smooth back and forth rhythms. Her husband took her hand. Holding it gently, he stroked one of her fingers from knuckle to tip.

"Mother, how can I serve you?" he asked her lovingly. He wished to remove her suffering.

She replied, "My dear, you have done all that is required of you. The Lord, now, will have to ease my pain." She paused, wiping her face with a lacy handkerchief. "And you? What may I do to comfort you, husband?" she asked.

"Sweet woman, through you God gave me my lovely Twila...and precious Vilet." He stroked her hand again. "You rest now, woman. Let me serve you in this time."

"What of the person who did this?" she inquired.

"The Lord will deal with him."

"But, Brother, is it not in service to the Lord to protect others from being harmed?" she pleaded.

He paused and thought. For it was always wise to reflect first, rather than speak words of which you were uncertain. "It is." He considered all of the weak in his village. Except when the Union took some of their men, never before had such a crime been committed upon their people. And certainly never against someone as vulnerable as sweet Twila. What would prevent him from doing it again? Conflicted by the command to *turn the other cheek,* he began to give deep consideration to seeing that the criminal be stopped. He could not know that, close by, a girl in soldier's garb considered the same thing.

Della made her way through the encampment. Trying to look natural, she moved around searching. Her eyes focused on everyone within a few feet, then over their heads and beyond. No sign of John could be found. No sign of that swine, Burdock. Discouraged, she glanced downward for a moment. And upon raising her head, she came face to face with none other than Clyde Diggs and Caleb Henry, dogs in their own right.

"Well, look who it is," one of them said in a smarmy way. "If it ain't the little friend of the girl killer." He laughed like the idiot he was.

"What are you talking about?" Della asked him, afraid to hear his answer.

He replied, "You *got* to be foolin' me!" He looked at his friend while slapping his own knee, bending over with laughter. "He don't know *nothing* about his friend, does he?" Now addressing Della, he snorted, "First you don't know that he actually *killed* Major General Thomas Stonewall Jackson! Now you claim you don't know that he cut that Mennonite girl's throat?! Everyone knows it!" He continued laughing and mocking. "Why, they're looking for him now! And when they find him…oh, it ain't gonna be good. It ain't gonna be good."

Her heart raced in her chest. "You two are a couple of fools if I ever saw them."

The other replied, "We'll see who's the fool when

Cumfrey gets strung up…er shot." He guffawed and addressed his friend. "Fact, I'm gonna put in to be on his firin squad!" He looked at Della again. "You just watch me." Speaking to his friend, he said, "We shoulda hung him back in Bladen."

Infuriated, she stormed away from them, then began to run.

He yelled toward her back, "You just watch! I'll hit him square between the…"

His voice faded as she got farther away.

Lord, please show me where to go. She prayed in her head. *Lead me to John, Lord. I need to find him.*

She had covered every inch of the camp. He was not there, it was clear to her. Remembering the way he ran, she entered the woods and began moving in that direction. She moved stealthily for the first ten yards or so, wanting to remain unnoticed. And once out of earshot, she called for him. "John. John." No answer returned, and she moved deeper into the woods, and into the higher elevations.

She searched for a path, but found none. Just untouched woodlands as far as she could see. And if anyone was looking for him, it was a surprise to her. She had been about in the forest for more than an hour and had seen no evidence of any search posse. Her legs began to ache, and she realized that the encampment was far below her. In fact, she could see the tops of the houses on the Mennonite hill. "John!" she called to him, but she heard only silence.

Dried leaves made a thick blanket beneath her feet, and living green leaves rustled in the breeze above. If it were not for the circumstances, she would have been utterly taken aback by the beauty of the woods. It was exactly the kind of place she loved, so much like Boone, so much like the days before all this sadness. But, not stopping to take it in, she pressed deeper into the overgrowth searching for the boy she loved.

Chapter Eighteen

A strong oak stood in the middle of the forest. It had seen the days of the Revolution and now, more than a hundred years later, it bore witness to this war. With one hand on it, feeling its massiveness, John followed its trunk upward with his eyes. So high it was dizzying. In its old age, it towered above all the others, no doubt coming closer to heaven than anything else he could think of. "This is the one," he quietly said to himself.

He began carving. First the name, and then a heart big enough to go around it. Working, he cried and spoke to his lost love. "Twila, dear, I'm so sorry I wasn't man enough to tell you. All I can give you now is this." The muscles in his arms flexed as he dug into the flesh of the tree. "I'm sorry if I brought this upon you." He said no more until he was finished. "My heart, Twila. It's yours. It will be here long after I am gone." His whole body ached with grief. And his lungs hurt from the sobbing. Exhausted, he lay at the foot of the great oak and fell into slumber.

Almost crying now, Della called to him. "John? John!" But no reply came. She began to fear the worst, thinking that she might come upon his body lying in the leaves or swinging from a tree. She had made her way into dense woods, and she stepped carefully, feeling her way around tree trunks, and ducking under low-hanging branches. A sticker bush caught her arm. "Ouch!" Using her finger, she wiped the blood and rubbed it away into her palm.

Chkchhkkhhchkchhkchkk. She looked up in search of the source of the familiar sound. A timber rattler. She had seen Zebediah shoot a few back in Boone, and she slowly readied her rifle, thinking that a snake would be a fitting first shot. For she had plans to fire upon a couple of snakes who walked upright. Surely this one was less deserving of what he was about to get. She took aim. *Bang!!!* Backing off, she coughed, waving the dark cloud away with her arms.

When the smoke cleared, his remains were visible. One long headless piece of rattler lay still on the ground. The toothy head blasted apart in bits and pieces too small to be found. She had proved herself to be a good shot--at least with snakes. *Good food for some worms,* she thought.

John's head sprang up and looked around. Panicked and breathing hard, he cried, "Jesus, they're looking for me!" Wasting no time, he got up and ran, away from the sound of the shot, as fast as his tired legs would take him. Not far. But surely far enough that he would not be seen by whoever held that gun.

Some distance away from him, Della continued her search, making her way through the thick brush. With her eyes wide open for any more snakes, she stepped carefully. Against the dull colors of the forest, something glistened for a moment then disappeared when she moved. She leaned left and right, hoping to see the glimmer again. For a split second, it shone, and she was upon it in a moment. Bending, she pushed aside some debris. The shiny blade revealed itself, almost blinding her with a concentrated glint of the setting sun. "John," she said to herself.

Relieved to see no blood on the blade, she stood examining it closely. She ran her fingers gently along the handle, knowing that it had been recently touched by the one she loved. She felt heat. He must be near. And she surveyed the area. From the corner of her eye, something stood out against a large tree. So she moved closer, jaw hanging open. Her small hands touched the carving, feeling every part of it--first the heart, then the name. Not her name. She wouldn't have expected it to be, but the image now confirmed the cold reality. Her love did not love her, not that way.

A hard slam knocked her to the ground. Finding herself pinned by the shoulders, she looked up. The hit didn't matter. It was the face she had been looking for. "John!"

Upon her, he was angry like she had never seen him. He breathed hard, spraying her with spit as he demanded, "Why did you do it?! Why did you hurt her?!"

Della yelled back, "Do what?! What are you saying?!"

He backed off a little. "You *know* what I'm sayin! You killed Twila! You never had no girl like her! You was jealous that I had her, and you took her from me!" He recoiled, covering his face as he sobbed. "Why'd you do it? Why'd you do it?"

"God, no. No!" She considered that this whole thing must be her imagination. But, feeling the physical pain of being knocked to the hard ground and the wetness on her face, she knew. Certainly this was no dream. "John, no!" Tears now streamed down, her heart breaking for multiple reasons. *John loved Twila. Twila was dead. And he was blaming Della.*

John glared at his former friend. "Why should I believe anything you say?" His voice was running down like a music box that needed rewinding.

Thankful just to have him talking to her, she moved closer and whispered, hoping to keep the little bit of trust he was offering. "Have I ever been dishonest to you?" She wished she had said it differently. For, she knew she *had* been. Indeed, their whole relationship had been a lie. She thought, *you don't even know who I am.*

Trying hard to keep her femaleness concealed, she pleaded. "Please. Please, John. You are my friend." She paused, wiping her red eyes and trying to catch her breath. Wanting to say *I love you*, she told him, "I care for you, John. Please." She extended her hand, palm up. He accepted it and shook, signifying that they were, once again, friends.

But she wasted no time on romantic notions. "John, there's rumors at the camp."

"About what?" he asked.

"About you. About Twila," she told him.

"I don't get it." But he really did.

So she elaborated. "They think you did it, John."

Flabbergasted, he asked, "What?! Me?! They think I killed her." This he said as a statement, in an *it figures* tone. Trying to make sense of what he just heard, he hung his head, shaking it in disbelief.

"Diggs and Henry, they told me that they were looking for you." She spoke remorsefully, her heart breaking.

He stared into nowhere, a look of surrender on his face. "I knew it would end this way." He spoke softly. " I knew it. No good could ever come of my life. I might as well go back and give myself up."

"What are you saying?!" Close to his face now, she stared him in the eye. "You are *not* gonna do that! No!"

"Why not? They're gonna find me an kill me anyway."

She retorted, "And what about the real killer?! If you let them put the blame on you, he'll go free!"

"So," he told her, giving up.

"So?" she mocked. "You're gonna let the dog that killed Twila get away with it? So he can do it again?!"

He squeezed and rubbed his face with his hand, distorting it as he considered her words. He knew that Cotton was right.

Della continued. "John, there's more."

Sarcastically, he asked his friend, "What more could there be? Tell me. I find out that this beautiful angel has feelings for me. That night, I'm in heaven, heaven I tell you! And in the morning it's all over. She's gone." He looked in Della's eyes. "Gone, Cotton." He paused, "So what more you got to tell me? Go ahead. It can't get no worse." Grinding his jaw closed, he fought back the tears and waited for a reply.

"I think I know who did it."

Nauseated, John leaned in and whispered angrily. "Who was it? You tell me! I'll kill him! I'll kill the bastard!"

Wasting no time, she blurted out a name. "Burdock."

He sat up, eyes scanning back and forth as the rest of him remained still, thinking. "Why? Why do you think that, Cotton?"

"He's a violent man, John," she told him.

"He is." John agreed. After a thoughtful pause, he added, "but there's plenty of violent men round here."

Hoping he would stop this line of questioning, she said, "But not like him." She whispered and leaned in for emphasis.

132

"He's evil, John. I'm telling you, he's plain evil."

Considering that Cotton might be right, he asked, "So what do you reckon I do?"

Della had always been quick-witted, but John proposed a vexing question. *What would they do?* "You can't go back there. Not now."

He just listened, letting the sharper of the two devise a plan.

She talked until the sun was low in the sky and the woods became shadowy blue. Then she handed her rifle, and what he needed to fire it, to John and made her way down the mountain, hoping to come out somewhere near the camp.

Chapter Nineteen

When the sun rose on the mountains and the valley, Della lay wrapped in her bedroll near the ashes of the night's campfire. Some others lay sleeping, and some moved around getting about the day's business. Three figures in wide-brimmed hats slowly descended the hillside. It was the first such visit since the awful discovery and, by the look of it, this would not be a hospitality mission. No women and no baskets. No mouth-watering smells in the air. And no Twila.

Eyes were upon them as they entered the camp, but they acknowledged no one. Their gazes focused straight ahead, they approached a large tent, indeed the tent of the Commanding Officer of the Division. They gave no prior notice, but he had been expecting them. Respectfully, he received them upon their arrival.

The duty rested on Twila's father, and his companions remained silent, present only in support of their brother. "Sir, thank you for receiving us."

Gentlemanly, he responded, "Certainly, sir. Please sit down." He motioned toward the only other chair, adding, "I apologize for the lack of accommodations. What can I do for you?"

"Our village suffered a terrible loss a few nights ago. *I...*" he stressed, "suffered a terrible loss."

The Officer said nothing, but nodded and listened.

"I have received knowledge of evidence, sir. Evidence that may be of use to you...in finding the criminal." He paused for a reply.

The Officer said nothing, but covered his mouth with his hand, waiting for the man to speak.

"My daughter." He stopped to collect himself, but remained outwardly stoic. "My daughter Twila. She scratched something into the soil before she passed."

Perfectly still and attentive, he told him, "I'm listening."

"A name. *John.*" He added. "The night that it happened I saw him with her. I saw a knife in his belt."

"I beg your pardon, sir." He spoke with the utmost respect. "We have many soldiers bearing that name. Can you give me his surname?"

Twila's father shook his head. "He had been coming to my wife each morning...for salve. When you people arrived, he had grievous poison ivy. She dressed his face for him five or six days. He is but a mere boy."

"Sir, I thank you." He gently placed his hand on the man's shoulder. "The words escape me. I am so terribly sorry for your loss." The last thing he said was, "Rest assured that the guilty will be served justice."

The father nodded solemnly. "Good day, sir." All three tipped their hats and slowly returned from whence they came.

When they were out of earshot, the Officer called out, "Farnsworth."

Lieutenant Daniel Farnsworth would be given the task of collecting information on the suspected murderer. He would also oversee any efforts to locate him and bring him under arrest. Farnsworth had proven himself adept at such missions. But his tongue was loose.

Before long, word had spread throughout the encampment. The dying girl had implicated John. A posse would be formed immediately. For the victim herself had pointed the finger. Knowing the accused, and having known the victim, Della understood the scrawled message in a way that the others didn't. For, she too was a young lady. And she knew the kind of sentiments that John could elicit--even from someone so close to death. She couldn't imagine that she would do it any differently. So, the meaning of the message was clear to her. A final testament of love. The cold irony being that it placed guilt upon the very one the dying girl sought to comfort. So, for John, and for Twila, Della sought to right the wrong.

Farnsworth selected two men for the impending search. The highest ranking of the two was a Corporal, smart and respected among his peers. The other was a Private, a capable young man known for his ability to follow orders well. But the quandary lay in finding the right addition to the pair. Generally, Farnsworth found success in a system of balances. That is, the posse functioned as one small unit. And he found it best to equip it with men of extremes. What he lacked now was someone with a natural inclination to hunt a man down. Someone able to view the wanted individual as an animal. For this was often a necessary element to apprehending a criminal. Contemplating his decision, three or four came to mind. After careful consideration, he settled on one. Confident that he would temper the humanity of the other two, he would be the right man for the job. And there he was, not too far away. "Private Burdock, may I have a word with you?"

Completely fake, but fooling no one, he greeted his superior. "Certainly, Sir. What can I do for yih?"

"I need another man, Burdock, to locate and return John Cumfrey."

Keeping a straight face, inside he felt like he had died and gone to asshole heaven, though there is no such place. "How does that involve me, Lieutenant?" he asked, knowing full well the gist of the conversation. He had a throat full of phlegm, but wanting to appear civilized, he didn't spit. He just sucked in his snot, making a snorting sound. For Farnsworth, it signified that Burdock was just the right kind of lowlife for the job.

He told him, "Be ready within the hour. Report to my tent."

"Yes, *Sir!*" Burdock answered.

Chapter Twenty

It was past noon, and the search posse had been gone for several hours. The camp bustled. Almost every soul riled up: many with excitement stemming from the hunt for Cumfrey, that killer of both important and gentle people. Others anxious with thoughts of the resuming march. Energy permeated the grounds. So, Della did not stand out when she approached the tent, the same one that had been visited by the Mennonites that morning.

Standing just outside the enclosure, she addressed him. "Sir. Pardon me."

Surprised and affronted, the Officer replied, "Boy, whatever it is, I have not the time." He continued what he was doing, paying the soldier no mind.

"I apologize for the interruption, sir." She took a couple of small steps closer to him.

"Boy, you're a bold one." He paused and looked her in the eye. "Whatever your concern is, I ask that you take it elsewhere!" Shuffling through some papers, he tried again to ignore the intruder, mumbling to himself. "I have men useless with Putrid Fever, an imminent march, and the blood of a Mennonite girl on my hands..."

Della persisted. "That is what I've come about, Sir."

Annoyed, but now slightly interested, he looked at her. Speaking slowly and purposefully, he inquired, "You've come about *what*, soldier?"

"The girl. I've come about the girl."

Impatient, he told her, "I'll give you a moment of my time, boy, and no more. I suggest you spit it out, or leave me."

She continued, no longer beating around the bush. "John Cumfrey didn't do it."

He squinted his eyes at her.

"I know who did it. It was not Cumfrey."

"Tell me what information you have, son." Though irritated with his overload of concerns, a part of him was struck by the soldier's seeming sincerity. And, oddly, there was something about the young man that conjured images of his own beloved child--a daughter. He sat down, resting his jaw on curled knuckles.

Relieved to have his full attention, Della said, "The one who did it also assailed me, sir. Twice. And he carries a dagger, sir, which I have seen him sharpening many times."

"Many of these men carry knives. That does not render a

man a killer," he pointed out. "Nor does keeping it sharp."

She went on. "Yes. But, he assailed me. Twice, sir," she restated.

"In what way did he assail you, and why did this go unreported?" he demanded.

She answered, "He grabbed me around the throat, Sir. He threw me to the ground, and threatened me with his knife."

"And if this be the case, why did you not file a report with your superior? I've seen no such report!"

Thinking quickly, she replied, "I thought it best to let the matter go, Colonel."

"Let the matter go," he mimicked angrily. "You waste my time, boy. I have no time for speculation. Give me a name, or some hard fact, or dismiss yourself!"

She answered in a word. "Burdock."

He remembered his own encounter with the man, his reeking breath and horrible snorting. Ordinarily a factual man, the suggestion seemed plausible, and the Officer considered it before speaking again. "Son, you must give me more. I cannot take action on mere suggestions. I have been given evidence which is contrary to what you are telling me."

She stared at him, unsure of how to reply. "There can be no evidence of what is not so, Sir."

Impressed now by the young man's apparent wisdom, he continued to engage. "Do you not consider it evidence that the killer's name was transcribed into the earth by the girl's own hand?"

"Not the *killer's* name, Sir," she stated.

Mocking again, he said, "Not the killer's name? Then whose name do you propose it was?"

"The one she loved, Sir."

He made an ugly face, the kind a person makes when realizing that they may have overlooked something very important.

Crouching behind a rock, John listened for footsteps. He had been in the same spot for hours. Still lamenting Twila, he now had additional concerns. Cotton had given him a reason to stay alive, and now he aimed to do so. But it seemed no easy feat. He just hoped that the rumors were wrong. Hiding out in the woods alone was one thing. Being hunted was a whole other situation--and one he'd rather avoid.

On foot, Farnsworth's motley group of men cut thoughtfully through the woods. While designated hunters, this was a war. At any moment, even a hunter could find himself the hunted, flanked and outnumbered, indeed outgunned, by Union devils. So they moved slowly keeping watch for snakes, yankees, and John Cumfrey. So far none of those had surfaced.

Burdock glugged some water from his canteen. He let some of it cover his face then, spreading it around his mug, he shook like a wet dog. "I can smell him. He's not too far off," he informed the other two.

The older one, appointed by Farnsworth the leader, said nothing but pictured Burdock a rabid dog on the prowl.

"It'll be nice to get my hands on that boy," Burdock mumbled.

The one in charge instructed him, "Lieutenant Farnsworth requested that we return him unharmed."

Burdock made a nasty face at him and rebutted, "I believe the main purpose of this posse is to apprehend a killer. That's what I intend to do. The *unharmed* part, I consider that to be optional."

The leader thought it best to remain quiet. For, it was imprudent to try to reason with the unreasonable. But he took note of Burdock's coarse disposition and prepared himself for what trouble it might present. It crossed his mind that such people often hang themselves with their own stupidity. So he let the comment slide and continued on his mission.

After hours of quiet, some unusual noise caught John's attention. His eyes shifted back and forth as he listened. Slowly he turned and rose from his post, peeking carefully over the top of the rock. He saw nothing. But he knew what he heard. With bent knees and hunched back, he moved away as quickly as he could without being detected.

With ears keen like a wolf's, Burdock was alerted. He said nothing, but readied his musket and moved swiftly in the direction from whence the sound came. The others followed right behind.

"There's the little bastard!" Burdock growled. He took aim. He shot as the barrel of his gun was violently pulled down, blowing a dusty hole in the earth in front of them.

"Don't! *I've* been assigned the duty of overseeing this search! I'll not have you blatantly violating orders!" the leader yelled. "We'll attempt to bring him back unharmed and alive!" He paused, making eye contact with the cur of a man, asserting himself as the Alpha. Stressing the word *Private,* he demanded, "Am I understood, Private Burdock?!"

His voice rumbled back resentfully. "Loud and clear." He pulled away, mumbling to himself, "you son of a bitch."

While the two sparred, the youngest kept on Cumfrey's trail. Ten yards or so in front of his companions, he turned toward them and quietly motioned. "Come on. I see him," he whispered.

From somewhere inside him John found the nerve to pause and look behind. He saw the boy, close to his own age, musket in hand. Fueled by pure terror, he bolted--and his pursuers did the same.

"No! No!" He yelled as he ran. "Don't shoot! Don't kill me! I didn't kill her! I didn't do it!"

Wheezing, exhausted, he was brought down by the young soldier, his shoulders pinned to the ground.

"I didn't do it!" His words wound down as he began to sob. "I swear. I didn't do it. I didn't." He opened his eyes, blurred with tears and could make out a familiar figure before him.

With his musket pointed at John's chest, Burdock grunted, "And if you didn't?" Stressing the word *who,* he asked, "Then who did?"

Chapter Twenty-One

On the same day that John and Della arrived at the encampment in Harrisonburg, Josiah Jackson exited a railroad train in Fredericksburg. There he would join the Infantry of the Army of Northern Virginia. And it was not long before he found himself on the move again. After Chancellorsville, Lee sought to advance his army northward. And with thousands of others, Cavalry and Infantry, Jackson made his way in the direction of Brandy Station.

The growing concentration of Confederate troops in and around Culpeper indicated a probable raid on Union supply lines, and the blue trailed the gray northward. Josiah Jackson could not know that about fifty miles to his west, camped in Harrisonburg, another enemy pursued him. But for now, there was another fool in her crosshairs.

The posse came down the mountainside with their captive, feeling victorious. Finding it remarkably entertaining,

Burdock taunted John. "Enjoy yer walk boy. It'll be one a yer last."

The words fell hard on him, but he said nothing. For anything would surely be the wrong thing, and probably enough for Burdock to shut him up permanently. So he remained quiet, careful not to rile the killer escorting him.

"Wanna hear how they knowed it was you?" he asked. He intended to tell him, either way. "That poor girl wrote yer filthy name on the ground while she lay dying." He took extreme pleasure in delivering this statement. He wondered if it would be the one to break John's silence. It was not. But inside the boy swirled a torrent of emotion. *A wretch like him had no right to be talking about a sweet girl like Twila.* It sickened him that he had to listen to the scum that killed her. And it sickened him that the killer had authority over him. *Not for long,* he prayed.

And in the midst of the angst, the bittersweet knowledge of her goodbye. For she must have loved him. Surely she loved him--if her dying thoughts went to him. And as her last blood and breath left her, she lay in the dirt, writing her first and last love letter to him. To him.

Farnsworth stood outside the tent. Erect and tall, he had the look of military regality as he watched for signs of his search party. He had no reason to believe that they would return empty-handed. And he was proven correct when, at last, they appeared with one additional person. Putting up no resistance, John walked alongside his captors, hands bound in front of him.

Entering the camp, many eyes were upon them. John lifted his head. *Where is he?* he thought, looking around for Cotton. But his friend was nowhere to be seen. His heart sank. He worried that Cotton had somehow been implicated. Or perhaps, he thought, a copperhead bit him on the way down the mountain. Whatever the case, it seemed that the plan had gone awry. John was crestfallen and resigned to surrender.

The leader handed John's seized rifle to Farnsworth. "He had this with him, Sir."

"Thank you, men," he replied, guiding Cumfrey into the tent with the barrel at his back. "Job well done," he added as he dismissed the three. And he disappeared into the tent with the prisoner in tow.

"Private John Cumfrey, Sir." Farnsworth addressed his superior.

"Well done, Lieutenant. I'll take custody of him now. You are dismissed." Farnsworth knew this to mean *Get out of my tent, you idiot.* And he left.

"Private," the Officer called.

John looked up, surprised by the tone with which he was being addressed. But, indeed it was someone else being summoned.

"Cotton," he gasped, unsure of what to make of it. Why was his friend inside the Colonel's tent? Was this a good thing?

Or was it a bad thing? Whatever the case, he knew how it felt to see him.

"Untie him," the Officer quietly instructed Della.

How good it felt to touch him. She hid her desires. Wanting to embrace him, she brushed imaginary dust off of his shoulder instead.

A large flap of canvas was pulled down, shielding them from curious onlookers. The Officer knew that John had been through a rough few days, and he gestured for him to sit down in the other chair. "Cumfrey, I apologize for your..." He paused, searching for the right word to use. "...the way in which you were retrieved. Be advised that absence without leave is a violation of your duties here, and subject to whatever penalty I choose to impose."

"I'm sorry, s..."

The Officer interrupted, "I had been given information which, I believed, pointed to your guilt in the death of the Mennonite girl..."

John gulped nervously.

He continued. "But is has come to my attention..." He looked at Della. "...that another party is responsible, and that you are innocent in this matter." He paused and searched John's face for a response. "I need your sworn statement to this end. I cannot take further action in your release without it."

"I'm innocent, Sir," he stated.

"Wait." The Officer stopped him, walking to a small table at the back of the enclosure. He returned holding a large Bible. John had never seen one with gilded pages before, and he considered it an honor to lay his hand upon it. "Now tell me, in your own words, what connection you have to the murder of this girl."

With his right hand shaking in the air, John said, "I have no connection to the murder of my sweet Twila."

"And is it your claim to be fully innocent of the charge of murder?"

"I am fully innocent," John said. And he almost passed out with relief.

Chapter Twenty-Two

There was one full day left before the brigade of men at Harrisonburg would embark on another northbound march. Restlessness abounded across the camp. Again the soldiers prepared to say goodbye to what had become familiar surroundings. Still torn with emotion, John welcomed the idea of departing from a place now connected to such sadness. But he also struggled with the melancholia of never again seeing the place where his first love flowered and perished. It amazed him that such a war could rage within another war. And within that war, a war of his heart. *Lord, let me be free of this place. But, Lord, let me see it once again.*

A plan was in place for him. He was to act the part of a guilty man while the real killer was given enough rope--enough to hang himself with. And if the plan failed, the trouble would rest on the Commanding Officer. For the new evidence and John's proclamation of innocence was enough for the Colonel, and he would see to it that an innocent man not be punished for the crimes of another. Bringing justice to the guilty was another matter altogether.

Light rain fell in the morning. Soldiers ate the last meal that they would have there. Many feared that it might be their last meal anywhere. Burdock tied his bedroll, feeling rejuvenated. As usual, he had stepped in shit and come out smelling like a rose. Collecting his supplies and packing them for the journey ahead, he inwardly recounted his eventful stay. He had deflowered that soldier girl, given swift justice to the one who rejected his advances, and now John Cumfrey's feet would soon be kicking while he hung under a branch. Burdock held his head up with pride. He knew for sure that they never woulda caught the little bastard without him.

"Private Burdock," a voice beckoned. The Commanding Officer stood before him. "I wanted to personally thank you for your work in apprehending John Cumfrey."

It's about time they saw the value in me, he thought to himself. "Well, it wasn't easy work, Sir."

"No, bringing the guilty to justice is never easy, Mr. Burdock."

He stood there, soaking it all in, awaiting the next compliment.

"In light of your outstanding service, I think it only fitting to involve you in the process of bringing this case to a close.

That is, seeing that justice is served." He kept his composure, knowing that he looked into the eyes of a killer.

Burdock scratched his chin. "In what way, sir?" He imagined himself tying the hangman's knot and kicking away the barrel under Cumfrey's feet.

"I have received his spoken confession. All that remains now is to take a report of the murder itself."

Burdock found the idea utterly fascinating. The crazy loon. He confessed! Just like that crazy girl! She'd rather die than take a flourishing! He thought, *"Boy, if those two weren't made for each other!"*

The Officer continued, "Once we have documented the additional evidence, the guilty party will receive swift justice."

Amused by the notion, Burdock replied, "Swift justice is the only justice, Sir."

"Indeed," he answered. "You will lead a small group to escort him to the place of the murder. There you will take his statements on the details of the crime."

"It would be my privilege, Sir," he said, in a smarmy way.

"Very well," the Officer said. "Report to my tent in one hour where you will collect him." He walked away. Turning for one last look, he added, "The guilty believes that the forthcoming evidence will lessen his sentence. Say nothing about his fate. Act swiftly, Burdock. Justice must be executed today."

Almost every one of his nasty teeth were visible as he

packed his things, grinning. For he had always known that he was so much smarter than other people. But today was truly a banner day. Everything was going his way, and all it required was that he be his own natural, highly intelligent, self. Yes, today seemed the culmination of all of his fine decision-making abilities. Nothing could ruin this day. Not the rain. Nothing.

He looked at the others around him. "You sorry jackasses hear that? They want *me* to oversee the justice for that dead girl."

None of them so much as grunted in acknowledgement. Burdock hardly seemed the kind of man that should be delivering justice to anyone.

Angered by their indifference, he said, "Yea, you fools just stay quiet. My luck is changin. You won't find me sitting around your sorry campfire at the next bivouac. You mark my words." He spat at the ground, wiped his chin with his sleeve, and walked away leaving his belongings neatly packed for his departure. They looked at one another as if to say *And wouldn't that be nice?*

Less than an hour after his meeting with the Colonel, Burdock waited outside the Officer's tent, the look of pride still beaming on his leathery face. Within minutes Cumfrey emerged, his hands still bound with twine.

"Untie him," the Officer instructed. "You will take him to the murder scene where he will demonstrate to you his heinous actions. You will provide the evidence to me so I may make a full report."

Burdock nodded, grabbing John around the scruff of the neck. Not knowing how to read or write, he was glad that he would not be asked to transcribe a report himself. And what a waste of time reading or writing woulda been for him. It woulda made no difference whatsoever. He couldn't so much as write his name, and his future was as bright as any. Who knew what tomorrow might bring? Indeed, who knew what today might bring?

The Officer handed one of the soldiers a long piece of rope, stating, "When finished, the criminal must be bound again and returned to me." He nodded, as if they shared some secret.

Burdock, John, and three trustworthy soldiers made their way up the hill, many eyes fixed upon them. Some in the camp, and some in the village. Periodically, Burdock shoved his charge. More than once, John fell to his hands and knees then got back up. In his demented mind, Burdock pictured Jesus being led to the Crucifixion. And it made him feel that much more important.

Approaching the top of the hill, John hesitated, falling to the ground behind his escorts. "You get up, boy. I'm telling you now, get up!" Burdock demanded.

Unable to continue, the boy lay there.

Burdock kicked his side and yelled, "Get up, ya little bastard! Take what ya got comin to ya!" He kicked him again for good measure.

John said nothing. And Burdock became more infuriated with each moment, landing several hard blows.

"Stop," one soldier said, bending and placing himself between the boy and Burdock's forceful boot. "We'll remain to the task at hand, Private Burdock. Our duty is to lead him to the scene. I see no need to harm him any further."

He replied, "The Colonel made *me* the leader of this assignment, and it'll be up to *me* if I want to kick this worthless piece o shit!"

"Burdock, justice will be served in this case. Remain patient. The guilty will receive his punishment. I assure you of that."

He backed off. And John just lay on the ground, moaning.

The soldier nearest him continued, "I will deal with him. Carry on to the place, and the murderer will be there momentarily."

Flanked by the other two, Burdock led them. Making his way through the village he passed the house where the little girl was taken from her bed. Her parents watched from a window, shielding Vilet's eyes from whatever was transpiring. They lamented the evil that the warring English had brought to their world. They mourned what had been taken from them.

Some paces behind, John and his escort followed. Proud

to be leading, Burdock brought them to the end of the village and over a small knoll. Stopping at a particular spot, he turned and looked back. Dead in his tracks, John stood, glued to the ground, his eyes fixed on the earth beneath Burdock's feet.

"I'm waitin'!" he ordered. "Get over here and show us what you did to her!"

Dazed, John shook his head and remained still. Keeping it all inside, he surveyed the spot. *This is where my Twila died.*

Seeing tears streaming down the boy's face, Burdock became enraged. He stormed to him and grabbed the back of his neck, squeezing hard. Like the mad animal he was when he killed Twila, he frothed at the mouth, dragging John to the exact spot where she had been found. He shoved him down, and bits of dirt stuck to the side of the boy's wet face. He lay there, barely able to breathe.

"C'mon, boy! Show us what ya did to her before ya slit her throat! Show us…"

"That's enough!" another voice ordered. "Bind him and take him to the Colonel."

Blindsided, Burdock demanded an explanation. "What?! What the *hell* is goin on here?!" He tried to shake them off, putting up a violent fight, but the three were too much for him. And, within moments, he stood hunched over and gasping for air, still swearing. Burdock was unaware of what had taken place. Indeed, he had led them to the right location. Hidden out of view, it was known only by the ones who found her, those who had washed away her blood, a select few in on the set-up, and the killer himself. He had sealed his own fate. And John Cumfrey was now exonerated--if not in the death of Stonewall Jackson, at least in the death of the precious girl.

What Burdock had done in the dark, no human saw--none but himself and the one he killed. But many witnessed the scene as he stumbled down the hill, hands bound behind him. As requested, the guilty man was delivered to the Colonel. The Officer stood erect outside his tent, awaiting their arrival. "Fine work. Fine work, gentlemen."

Burdock tried to wrestle free. "You bastard! You son of a bitch!" He hurled no threats, knowing that they would be empty. "Rot in hell, you bastard!" He spat at the Colonel's feet. Struggling, he cursed them all. "Rot in hell, all of you!"

As Burdock continued his fight, the officer instructed, "String him up. Time is short." And he turned his back as they led him away.

Chapter Twenty-Three

Vultures circled again. The smell of death was strong at the encampment in Harrisonburg. They cut him down from the tree once he was good and dead. And they would have liked to leave him there to feed the hungry birds. But out of courtesy to the Mennonite people who had shown such kindness, and who had suffered at the hands of this dead wretch, they took him down and threw some soil over him. It would spare them an awful sight and a putrid stench. No tombstone was placed for him. For some people are better forgotten.

His belongings were unpacked and dispersed among the men who had put up with him. Most of it he had probably stolen from the dead, so what harm would it be for it to be stolen from him now that he was dead? And perhaps it would be stolen later should the new owner not make it through the next skirmish.

Della had watched the hanging. She saw them put the noose around his neck and hoist him upward. She saw the struggle when his feet, at last, left the ground and began to violently kick the air. And then nothing, just a lonesome quiet swinging. The breeze pushing him to and fro. And he would no longer be a threat. No longer a threat to the purity of young girls, or tightly held secrets. A sense of relief washed over Della when the life had finally left him.

But it was not complete relief. For the war still raged. And there was the concern she didn't want to imagine. Could that swine of a man have made her with child? *Dear God, no!* she prayed. She shuddered to think of it. Having a child out of marriage would be unspeakable itself. But what would she do? What would become of her if her belly started to swell while she lived this life of a boy, of a soldier? And what of Josiah Jackson? Would he never pay for what he had done to Zeb? She was determined, if through pure will, that there would be no child to thwart her mission. And somewhere deep within her, she trusted that her God would not curse her that way.

"Cotton," a voice quietly beckoned.

"John!" she exclaimed, trying not to seem too excited to see him. "It's over, John. They hung him."

He nodded at his friend, emptily. "I know. I knew what was comin." He had not followed Burdock down the hill, but instead sat at the scene for a little while. The gentle rain fell on him and he hung his head down, wiping his hands back and forth in the muddy earth where she had written his name. It was the same soil that soaked up her blood. He said goodbye to her and he walked away.

From the window in the brown house, Twila's mother and father watched the events. Burned into their minds were images of John being kicked. Of that violent man being dragged away. And of John, no longer bound, but walking free. Walking solemnly alone, something heavy on his heart. For he appeared the same as they felt. Like something precious had been stolen from him.

Della put her hand on John's shoulder. "I'm so sorry," she told him. "I know that you loved her." She looked at him, not knowing what else to say.

"I do, Cotton. I do love her," he said quietly.

"John," a familiar voice called from behind.

He turned, a look of shock on his face. Not knowing what to expect, he took one step backward and acknowledged her. "Yes, Ma'am."

Twila's mother spoke. "I believed that you took my daughter." She looked down, almost ashamed. "It felt wrong on my heart, and now I know the truth."

John stared at her, speechless. Though wet with rain, his face felt like it was on fire.

She continued. "My girl had affection for you. I can see why. You have a kind heart, John." She paused and removed something from her basket, holding it tightly in her hand as she spoke. "Twila wrote your name in the earth before she passed. I felt you ought know that. I see it now as her way of saying goodbye to you." She began to cry softly. "I want you to have this." She handed him the small parcel wrapped in white cloth. "It was hers. They found it where she died. Please keep it in good care. I pray that it keep you in good care." Stepping closer to him, she embraced his face with both her soft hands and stared at him for a moment, like a mother would do to her beloved child. "Perfect as a human face can be," she whispered.

As the rain subsided and the sun shone through the clouds, John's attention turned to the object in his hands, and he did not notice as the woman continued up the hill, away from him for the last time. Della stood close to him as he unfolded the cloth. In his hand, a tiny wooden cross.

Chapter Twenty-Four

It was early June 1863, and John and Della marched northward up the Shenandoah with more than a thousand men. Throughout the valley, many more moved separately in fits and spurts to avoid detection as much as was possible. Anticipating a Rebel invasion in the north, many Federals continued to move homeward, prepared for battle.

Each day the number of men grew. Lee continued to fortify his army, combining battalions of soldiers so that, once engaging the enemy, they would be a formidable foe. Only days before, the Confederacy met Union forces at Brandy Station near Culpeper. Shielded from detection by JEB Stuart's Cavalry, Josiah Jackson and the rest of Lee's Infantry escaped the bloodshed and now marched northward, ready to join thousands of Confederate counterparts in an assault on enemy territory. Like an over-farmed field, Virginia had been depleted and General Lee saw gains to be had in the north: food for the famished soldiers, much needed supplies, and the military advantage of seizing control of enemy soil. But first, there would be Union to be dealt with farther north in Virginia.

John and Della made it a point to stay within sight of one another on their march from Harrisonburg. Once again, they left behind the relative comfort of camp. For long periods of time, no words would be spoken. But occasionally, the silence was broken.

"I'm hungry," John told his friend.

"I know," she answered. After a pause, she added, "Better get used to it. We're back to one ration of salt pork and hard corn bread."

John thought of the lovely Twila and the tasty bounty she and her people shared. Almost able to read his mind, Della saw a certain look in his eyes and quickly jerked him elsewhere with her words.

"Stay close to me," she said. "I mean, let's stick together when it happens."

He knew what she meant. "Of course, Cotton. We'll cover each other." He looked over at her. "You've been a good friend to me, Cotton. Best I ever had. I'll never forget what you did for me in Harrisonburg."

She looked at him modestly, but inside she was hungry for more.

"You saved my life."

She replied, "God and your innocence saved your life, John. I was an instrument, that's all."

He went on. "Cotton? Have you ever thought about when the war ends? Where you gonna go? Where you wanna settle down and what you wanna do with yer life?"

Wishing she could tell him the full truth, she offered bits and pieces of it. "Sometimes," she said. "I wanna be married some day. I would love to be a..." She stopped herself. "I would like to have children."

"I haven't even thought about that," he answered. "I might a married Twila...and I reckon we might coulda had babies." He paused for a while, thinking. "But I guess that wasn't in the Lord's plan for me." He wasn't sure where that came from, but it felt quite natural flowing from his lips.

Della added, "I've known the Lord to keep His plans a secret until He's good and ready to reveal them."

"I guess you're right," John said. "But what's hidden will be revealed." He wasn't sure where that came from either, but he was pretty sure he had heard it somewhere once.

Cotton nodded, not sure what to think.

"Cotton?" John engaged his friend again.

"Mmmm?" she answered.

"I consider you like family."

A chill of excitement ran up her spine, and she shivered. No one noticed.

"I mean, if I had any family to speak of." Nervously rubbing his lower lip with his index finger, John added, "And now that I have someone like that, it would be important to me to be close to them in my life."

Della listened, hoping he would go on.

And he did. "I ain't never had a brother. And if I did, I know he wouldn't be no better than you. Bladen county means nothing to me. I got nothing there. The best thing I had was Diggs and Henry. And that ain't no more. Do you think the people of Boone would mind me? Do you think yer family would mind me, if I settled close to you and set up my life there? Nobody there knows who I am. And they don't know what I did...I mean what happened in Chancellorsville."

Containing her feelings, she replied. "John, no right-thinking person would mind having you around."

A reserved grin arose on his face. It was the first such expression she had seen on him since the night of their fight, the night that Twila died.

"It's settled then," John proclaimed. For the second time in his life, he felt like he belonged, like he was wanted. His spirits were lifted greatly, and it helped soothe his sorrow.

In early evening, the order to bivouac came. Though they were tired, the march had charged the soldiers with a renewed energy. After setting up temporary camp, they readied themselves for the likelihood of battle. For some, this meant attending to their weapons. For others, it meant lively conversation. It all depended upon what they believed the next day might bring. Those determined to stay alive prepared for the immediate future. And those thinking that death might be imminent determined themselves to enjoy the here and now. All of them implored God that night. *Protect me Lord. If I die, take my soul, Lord. Help me to be brave, Lord.*

Chapter Twenty-Five

Word had come, that morning, that the Confederacy had engaged with Union forces south of Winchester. The Federals had maintained control of that city since 1862, and Lee sought to retake it and the many contraband soldiers there assisting the Union efforts.

It was there that Josiah Jackson experienced the confusion and terror of battle for the first time. Running on adrenaline, he charged when told to charge, and retreated when told to retreat. The loud and bleeding battlefield seemed the only environment in which he would follow orders. And he did it well. And he was still alive.

As the Confederate Army fought to overtake the firmly bulwarked Union in Winchester, Josiah made it a point of avoiding the front line. Whoever stood in front of him was a sort of flesh shield. And if the dividing of skirmish lines left him open and vulnerable in an end position, he sloppily made his way to the middle where there were more men who could serve as barriers, human ramparts, between him and the bullets. And this cowardly behavior served him well, as it had all his life.

From Star Fort, Howitzers boomed. To Jackson's left, a hot ball rocketed into the crowd, taking down five men. They flew backward onto each other like dominoes and then fell still. Jackson fired at the enemy trenches, hoping that he had hit some evil yank. Maybe two if he was lucky. Breathing was hard with the running and the smoke in his lungs. But he kept on, determined not to let some Union devil take his life from him. And if they would, well he would take as many as he could with him to hell.

He thought to himself while in the middle of it all. He recounted how his Brigade had proudly uprooted Union picket soldiers somewhere around Front Royal. *The way those cowards ran.* And now heavy artillery sounded back and forth around him, and he was determined that he would not be caught in any crossfire. Cannon or rifle or otherwise.

"Forward!" his Commander called out, barely heard above the fire. Josiah sprinted forward, as usual behind another man. And before he could think about it, they were upon the enemy, each side charging with bayonets lowered. Metal points came from every direction. In front of Jackson, a Confederate went down, but not before firing at the enemy in his way. With no one blocking him and nowhere to go, Josiah advanced. On the ground below, a boy of no more than sixteen summers lay looking up at him, a bullet in his body. He squeezed his arm, trying to stop the bleeding and the burning. He prayed to God that he would be shown mercy, somehow.

But mercy was something that eluded Josiah. He aimed his bayonet downward, hovering over the child's neck, for just long enough to strike some terror in the fallen boy. He grunted like a bear, then slammed it downward so forcefully that it stuck in the Virginia red clay. A warm spray covered his face as he pulled back his weapon. He then pressed forward looking for someone else to kill. And he took several before the Federals again retreated. When the smoke cleared, and the Union were out of sight, the Commander could be heard, "Good work, men! Good work!"

As Providence would have it, Della Cotton marched into a war zone not knowing that an enemy greater than the Union was enjoying the taste of blood only a few short miles away.

"Get in the hole!" a Sergeant hollered.

How incredible it seemed to feel so vulnerable, so open to attack while surrounded by thousands of brothers in arms. But that is how it felt for her, and she ran to the abandoned trenches while gunfire cracked over her head.

"John! John!" She pulled him close and forced him low into the bulwark. "Stay down!" Cowering and shaking, she loaded her rifle. But her stature was too small to take aim over the top, and her disposition would not allow her to fire blindly.

"Stand on my back!" John ordered her.

Quizzically, she looked at him. But within seconds she was standing on his spine as he crouched in the bloody wet dirt. She asked God to forgive her for what she was about to do, and she took aim at any yankee visible and close enough to hit. In an attempt at mercy, she aimed for heads. To her own horror, she found herself to be a good shot on the battlefield. And with each casualty, John could hear her saying, "Dear Lord, forgive me."

Crying isn't something that people tie to battles, but there was a lot of it going on in Winchester that day. Unable to stop and consider the human loss, the suffering, the destruction, Della continued firing from the trench. With tearful eyes, she took aim and fired again and again, stopping only to reload.

Full of fear, hunger, and pain, John sobbed beneath her feet thinking that, if he could just close his eyes tight enough, it might all go away. But it didn't.

After some time, the popping of rifles slowed, and the yelling subsided. Della breathed heavily, feeling as if there was not enough air in the world. Moving off of her friend, she collapsed next to him. Sweat and dirt mixed on her skin, making her almost unrecognizable. "Oh God." It took a long time to catch her breath. In between gasps, she spoke. "Are you alright?"

John didn't answer, but just stared ahead nodding. His

eyes wide with terror.

Some moaning and crying could be heard in the relative quiet following the engagement. It was only then that they noticed the dead occupying the trench with them. Some were their comrades, but some were Federals who had been killed earlier. No foul smell could be detected. Only the sulfurous smell of gunpowder. So Della imagined that they had not been there too long. She knew what death smelled like, and it had not settled in yet. She stayed crouched in the hole until the order came to get out.

"Stay close," she instructed John. John did, knife in hand. A new experience in many ways, this was the first time Della had seen so many people in one place. Through the sea of soldiers, she surveyed her surroundings as best she could. Trying to see the landscape, it was hard not to look at the bodies, though she tried. Inside, she lamented that she had been an instrument in the bloodshed. But there was no time for sorrow.

It was the first time among new soldiers that she had not searched for that face. That despicable face of Josiah Jackson. If only temporarily, his evil deed was overshadowed by her own murderous actions on the battlefield. Dead and dying men lay all around, and she wondered how many were lying there by her own hands.

Now, in the relative calm, women could be seen scattered throughout the fields, attending to the dying and checking the dead for signs of life. Black men lay among the dead, here and there. It would have been a surprise to Della, to see a Negro in uniform. But all the fallen looked the same, black or white, broken and bent on the battlefield. Indeed all of the faces were the same color. Dusty. Still now. No distinctions among them.

Chapter Twenty-Six

"The next skirmish…that's when we do it." With downward chin and shifting eyes, Diggs instructed his cohort. "It's bad enough he killed General Jackson, but to get away with killin' a girl…"

"I know," the other replied. "You sure nobody'll keer?"

"Care? Bout what? They'll prolly give us a blue medal…er whatever medal they give." They laughed stupidly.

There were so many men. For most, they need not hear an order. All that was required was to blindly follow all the others. And most did. For there was no resistance in moving with the masses. Over their heads, Della saw a group of weeping willows. They towered, new fronds swaying with the breeze. Her eyes followed them down to the marshy ground on which they grew. From the distance, it was hard to say for sure, but she thought she could make out the shadowy image of people strewn around, laying still as the gentle branches tickled their unresponsive bodies. And drummers drummed proudly as they continued to sweep through the Lower Valley.

Della did not recognize her surroundings. But she knew that she was moving north, chasing the Federals through Winchester. They pushed onward. And as they crossed the town, the sound of skirmishing could be heard. Westward from the streets, a large Brigade of Confederates joined them and moved north toward a place known as Apple Pie Ridge. In the innumerable army, fear subsided and was replaced by a feeling of being invincible, by a deep-rooted southern pride. With such numbers and such strength, surely they would be victorious. And in the eastern theater of the war, the Union would wave a white flag before the sun set.

The two brigades merged and appeared as one unified mass. Josiah Jackson made his way further toward the middle as he marched. And now far away from the place where she fired into the crowd, Della resumed her original mission. To find that bastard. The taste of blood gave fuel to her desire for justice. And, again, her eyes searched a new deluge of soldiers…for that face.

"Cotton," John called.

"Yea," she answered, not as a question like *what,* but more like the statement of *that's who I am.*

"What are you lookin' for?" he asked.

"Not looking for anything. Just looking. Some of these men will be dead today," she told him.

John chided her, "Be careful how loud you say that, Zeb." He went on, "Anyway, I pray to God it ain't so, but one of us or both of us could be dead before long."

Quickly and sternly she corrected him. "No!" For she knew that the God that had taken her this far would not now forsake her.

He knew that he had plucked a nerve, and he immediately dropped the subject. It wasn't a pleasant one anyway.

Della continued scanning the faces. *No, no, no* she thought as she went through them one by one. But she could not overcome the feeling she had. That feeling of the hairs sticking up on the back of your neck when someone is looking at you. The shiver you feel just before something bad is about to happen. And she had a feeling it had less to do with the war, and more to do with a personal matter.

Her eyes repeatedly worked their way right--for that is where the unchecked faces were. She looked there, among the unfamiliar, for something once familiar. And a shove from her left interrupted her search. John looked up at her from the ground.

"I'm sorry, Cotton." He got up quickly so as not to be stepped on.

Behind them, Diggs and Henry laughed and ridiculed.

"What's a matter, Cumfrey? New feet?!"

John ignored them as they continued mocking.

"You coward! Stupid fool! Even your friend, Cotton, here, gave up on ya! Whatcha gonna do now?! All alone in the world?!"

Della turned at them. Holding her rifle in two hands, she shoved it sideways into Diggs' chest. He stumbled backward and stuck his chin out at her.

"You do that agin, an you'll be sorry, Cotton." He gritted his rotten teeth when he said it.

She stopped and took mock aim at him with her weapon. "I think you'll be the sorry one." She said no more, knowing that she had made her point. And poor John, with only a knife to defend himself. It crossed her mind that he might be treated better by the Federals. Here he was taunted by his own. Surely there were dogs on both sides of this feud.

From the left, an unfamiliar soldier addressed the troublemakers. "What's that soldier's name?" He motioned toward John and Della.

Henry answered with a question. "Which one? The coward or the fool with the rifle?"

Jackson replied, "I guess the fool with the rifle."

He addressed his companion. "What's that boy's name agin?"

Diggs spat at the ground before saying it. "Cotton. It's

Cotton." He spat again to get the taste of the name out of his mouth.

Dumbfounded, Jackson asked, "What's his first name?"

"I don't know an I don't keer," he answered.

Jackson dropped back a little, but stayed close enough to keep an eye on him. He hadn't gotten a very good look, but there was a familiarity about the face. He waited and watched. *I was sure I killed him,* he thought. It couldn't be. Maybe it's a cousin or some other kin. One thing for sure, it was some relation. Of that he had no doubt.

Chapter Twenty-Seven

War changes people. It changes who they are from the inside out. From the morning to the evening that day, I tell you, that every man at that battle had changed. On the outside, not terribly so. Maybe a little dirtier, a little bloodier. But any man who was still alive had been altered in some way. For some, the death and violence stirred up anger and hatred, like stirring a cauldron of bubbling poison. It acted like lava inside a volcano about to burst. And, with pressure steadily building, it was just about to spew.

With each passing minute, Della's eyes grew more watchful. She searched every face in the crowd. And all the while, she herself was being watched. She looked behind and saw those idiots, Diggs and Henry. For good measure, she sneered. Behind them, a soldier ducked to the side just enough so that she could not see his face. Like a wolf whose curiosity is piqued by the movement of its prey, Della was driven to pursuit.

A lot like a bear following its dinner up a tree. Still keeping pace, she weaved around John and several others. And the prey weaved too.

"Zeb," John called. But no answer came. As his friend moved farther away, he followed. "Zeb! Zebediah!"

Not quite under his breath, Jackson gasped, "I'll be damned!" and he tried harder to remain unseen. Surely this Cotton boy would exact revenge upon him.

Neither noticed the voice calling over the crowd. "Ready cannon!"

As the Confederates turned their attention to the enemy, Della pushed her way through, following hers. There was no concern for the Federals and their Howitzers poised upon the hill. All of her attention was on the form clumsily moving away, and with too much purpose for her to ignore.

One after another Jackson shoved his fellow soldiers. "Move!" His fear intensified as he realized that his enemy was much closer than any yankee. And this one held a personal gripe. Pushing someone to the ground, he growled, "Hell out of my way!"

Della closed in. With the smooth barrel of her rifle in two hands, she smashed the butt down onto him, slamming the bones in his neck. Jackson tumbled to his knees and landed at the feet of the men around him.

In the mayhem, Della took aim and ordered, "Turn

around!"

He graveled, keeping his face close to the ground.

She repeated, "I *said* turn around!!"

Jackson slowly rolled over. His eyes followed the barrel of the rifle upward, and stopped on the face. It glared at him with ire, the like he had never before seen.

Della's chest boomed. Whether it was the cannons or the excitement of the moment, she did not know. But before her, justice awaited. The scum of all scum. Waiting to be served justice. And, with gun in hand, she stood tall ready to heap it upon him.

Many things will run through a man's mind when staring down the barrel of a gun. And you might think that Josiah Jackson's thoughts turned toward his escapades in the woods back in Boone. Or maybe toward repentance or a cry to God for salvation. But none of this was so. The face was all he could think about, and he couldn't take his eyes off of it. *That's not Zebediah Cotton,* he thought. *That ain't him.*

For what seemed an eternity, she dreamed of this moment. And now here it was, and she wanted to savor it, for just a few seconds before blowing his head off his shoulders. So she paused, hoping he would have enough time and gumption to feel terror or repentance or some uncomfortable feeling, the kind that Zebediah wasn't afforded.

"Where do you think you're going, Josiah?" She stopped

181

and waited for an answer.

Dumbfounded, John watched. Had it been anyone else, he might have tried to stop it. But he had known Cotton long enough to know that he was a wise person. Surely he knew what he was doing. Surely there was some good reason for taking aim at this person. So, while the war raged around them, John watched Della using her army-issued weapon to threaten a Confederate soldier.

In his smaller-than-normal brain, things began to click for Josiah Jackson. In a split second the wheels inside it turned, so much, so that Della could almost see the lights go on.

"I know you." He reached toward her, certain that he could talk his way out of it.

Bewildered, John looked on.

Jackson continued, changing his tone to one that a scoundrel might use to woo a naïve young lass. "C'mon now. You don't wanna hurt me."

Above the cannons and gunfire, she couldn't hear him. But she could make out the words as she watched his lying mouth move.

"Don't move you bastard," she ordered.

"C'mon now. We have a lot of catchin' up to do, De…"

She would have sooner shot his head off than let him say her name again. And she did. "That's for Zebediah!" She didn't even realize she had said it. "For Zebediah!" she said again as she turned and faced the reality around her.

And that was it. She didn't stop and look at what was left of him. She didn't ask God for forgiveness. She didn't even stop to wipe Josiah's blood and brains from her face. She just remained in the frenzy, aiming one by one at the enemy. And it wasn't such a hard thing now.

For a good while, the men of the Union and the men of the Confederacy exchanged gunfire. Little by little, the gray pushed northward while the blue backed up in the same direction. Now out of ammunition or the men to fire them, the cannons eventually quieted. And one with her brothers in arms, Della pressed northward hungry for yankee blood. She was down to her last few musket balls. And her powder was low. But she continued, methodical in her motions, picking them off one by one, and somehow avoiding all bullets fired in her direction. After she had fired the last shot, she looked around, still breathing hard.

"John!" Frantically searching, her eyes shot left and right. *Where is he?!* she asked herself. Running, she traced her path backward, looking through the crowd, calling to him. "John! John!!!" Her heart pounded in her chest as she ran, looking at every form, upright and fallen. "Oh God! Where is he? Where is he?!"

It was when she had reached the last line of the army, the end of her own violent hoarde, that she found him, only twenty feet or so from the remains of Josiah Jackson. There was no movement, only stillness. It was a sort of stillness that she had seen before. The stillness of the dead. The stillness of the almost dead.

She ran to him and fell to the ground. "No! No! John. No." Her screaming subsided into sobs, unheard over the chaos of the battlefield. Her head lay on his chest, his blood smearing onto her face and mingling with her tears. She squeezed his unresponsive hand and looked up to the heavens. "Oh Lord! No! No!" She lay back down beside him and cried, his hand still in hers. Warmth. It was warm. She knew what the cold of death felt like. Her love lay there but, my God, he was still warm.

They were behind now. Falling behind the advancing army of the south. She would carry him and catch up. Yes, she had no choice but to lift him and follow as best she could. Then, as if a message from God, one split second offered another option.

They had now fallen a good distance behind. And all eyes of the Confederacy were on the retreating Army of the Potomac. None looked back at them. They would not be missed. John's injuries had rendered him useless, and Della had no right being there in the first place. And it dawned on her that her mission had been completed. That cur, Jackson, was now dead. Probably burning in hell--where he belonged. There was no reason, now, to remain with them. She set her gaze south, deciding to seek help in the now Confederate-held city of Winchester.

Chapter Twenty-Eight

From a wooded area north of town, a man watched as Della dragged a body through the field. She had pictured herself throwing him over her shoulder, but reality would not allow it. Though thin, indeed bony with the starvation of the war, he was too heavy for her. For she, too, was malnourished and weaker than she had been when she first left Boone. But she was sure, in healthier times, she could have easily carried him.

The sound of gunfire can travel long distances. But it grew fainter and fainter still while Della took John's broken body southward through the valley. She fought discouragement. But the exhaustion was harder to overcome. Seeking to lighten her load, she laid down her pack and her rifle. Surely there would be some soldier who would put it to good use. And she looked forward to the moment when she could discard every last thing that had made her a soldier.

When she was far enough from her weapon, a voice

startled her. "Are you in need of help?"

She raised her head to locate the source of the very deep voice, a kind to which she was unaccustomed.

He repeated, "Are you in need of help, young man?"

She moved her lower jaw as she stared at him. But nothing came out.

"Do you not speak English?" he asked.

Finally, she found enough nerve to answer. "I need help. Yes. We need help." She was in no position to turn away such an offer, no matter who was making it.

The man bent down. He moved his large hands over John's middle, examining him, surveying his wounds. Lifting his shirt, two burned and bleeding holes were revealed. With care, the man pressed and felt the area with his fingers, like a bird feeling for a worm beneath the earth.

"I can feel this one. The other one, I don't know." He motioned to Della for help. "We need to turn him over."

Gently, they worked together, lifting him and turning him just far enough to see his back.

"That's bad." He showed her the damage. In his upper back, close to his shoulder, an exit hole. A large piece of flesh was missing. "But he might have a chance if we take care of it quickly."

He lifted the dying child into his arms and carried him as if he were a baby. Della walked beside him filled with conflicting emotions. Fear. And hope. In the distance, the battle had ended.

It was a scary thought for her, to be walking into the woods with a black man. But, for whatever reason, he was helping them. And she had no choice but to take her chances. He was large and, apparently, strong. But his countenance was gentle. And she followed hoping…no, *praying* for the best outcome.

Lord, if this man be an angel from You, then I thank you and I ask you to bless him. If he is a bad man, I pray you deliver us from him. Something told her to keep on. And while the man tirelessly walked with John's body resting in his arms, she followed. The field had vanished from sight, and Della had no idea where she was or where she was going. But she was beginning to believe it was the right way. And, for whatever reason, this man was her guide.

He kept a moderate pace, going slowly enough to maintain, and fast enough to hopefully spare the young man's life. It seemed he knew every step. It seemed a well-worn path to him. But, really, it was thick with overgrowth and well-hidden. All the better for remaining undetected when called-for.

Neither spoke. In silence they moved ahead, sharing a mission. And when they broke through the woods, the moonlight shone on the ground. A faint candlelight flickered from somewhere inside a clapboard house. And he broke the silence.

"Come." His voice assured her that it was alright. And she followed.

It had been a while since Della had been inside a house. And being there reminded her of Twila. And now John lay dying. Perhaps it was Providence. Perhaps it was meant for John to go to heaven to be with the one he longed for. Or maybe this was the Lord's way of punishing her. For the evil that she committed on the battlefield to men she did not know--and one she did know. She had been an instrument of death. And now, she feared, God would repay her with death. Standing in the unfamiliar place, she watched the man work. The moon was almost full and it cast enough light to reveal the proceedings to her.

"I need to remove the bullet," he quietly explained. "It'll be better for him to do it before he awakes…Lord willing he awakes."

He retrieved a knife from somewhere in the darkness. Della watched as he ran it back and forth through the candle flame, covering every part of it. Wiping it with a cloth, he waited a few seconds for it to cool then brought it to John's bared chest. Swiftly and with a surgeon's precision, he stuck the knife into the wound. In a moment, it emerged, and he used his other hand to ease out the dark lump that didn't belong inside a man. It made a clanking sound when he dropped it into a metal cup.

"You'll find a bucket over there," he said to her,

motioning into the dark room. "Get it."

She did as she was instructed, squinting her eyes to make her way through the small abode. "Here, Sir," she said, handing it to him.

He dunked a cloth into the water and tenderly wiped the wound, cleaning away blood and gunpowder. He used another cloth to dry the area. And Della watched closely, hopefully, as he applied some sort of dressing and covered it all up. When fully bandaged, he laid his big hand over John's chest and said a few quiet words with his head bowed down.

A sudden fatigue washed over Della. Her eyes became heavier and she called to the man. "Please, sir. Do you mind if I sleep?"

He said nothing, but guided her to a soft place on the floor and helped her to lay down. "Go to sleep, boy," he told her. And the bloody day ended.

When the new day arrived, Della was still sleeping. Sun shone through the window and landed on her body, but not yet on her face. Alone, she lay in the room, not much around her. But a light quilt of many colors had been placed over her. And it smelled of something familiar that aided her slumber.

The floor beneath her was made of roughly hewn planks. But they were softer than the hard ground of bivouac. The walls were the same clapboard of the outside, no layer in between. And two windows made of the bottoms of glass bottles flanked the front door, placed to allow a good amount of morning light. For it was the man's habit to read early in the day.

Inside the house, no evidence existed of the goings on of the previous evening. No knife, no bloody rags, no extricated bullet--and no wounded soldier. The now-empty bucket had been turned upside-down and left to dry near the hearth.

There was but one chair and one small table. A primitive looking shelf hung on the wall, home to ten or twelve loved volumes. A rope bed nestled in the back of the room. Four old posts marked the corners of the featherbed on top. At the foot of the bed, a wooden chest rested, a place for things which were necessary to life, but not on a daily basis.

The sun slowly moved higher in the sky, and the light made its way to Della's face. It made her nose twitch. And when it reached her eyes, they opened, crusted over with tears and blood. She spent a good minute blinking blurry eyes, wondering where she was. And then it all came back. She sat up on the floor and looked around, quietly, unsure of what to make of it. The man was nowhere in sight. And neither was John.

The thought crossed her mind that she might find her love outside, lying on the ground cold, and the strong black man digging a hole beside him. *No God, please* she begged. She stood not knowing what her next move would be. Instinctively, she walked toward the light. She rubbed her eyes clear and looked out the window. Walking with purpose, the man approached the house. The door opened next to her.

"Morning," he said.

"Morning," she replied. "Where's my friend?"

"He's resting," he told her.

"Where?" She wanted proof. She wanted to see him with his heart still beating.

"We'll eat. Then I'll take you to him," he informed her.

Something told her to trust him. She stood by the window and nodded. "After we eat," she said.

The man went outside and returned with a cut piece of tree trunk. He placed it near the table and motioned. "Sit. Please."

She did.

"Tell me about yourself," he instructed. She had never heard a black man speak so articulately. In fact, she couldn't remember having heard *any* man speak quite like him.

Trying not to seem so dumbstruck, she gave her reply. "I'm from Boone, North Carolina, sir."

He half-smiled. "Do people name their children in Boone?" As he talked, he worked a fire on the hearth.

Too nervous to get his joke, she answered, "Yessir, they do. Why?"

"No reason. I just thought it might be nice to know the name of my house guest." He half-chuckled.

Embarrassed, she told him, "My name is Cotton." For the

first time in a while, she considered offering her real name. But she erred on the side of caution and said, "Zebediah Cotton, sir."

"Well, it's good to know you Zebediah." He paused and stoked the fire. "And your friend?"

"John Cumfrey," she said, longing for him just by saying his name.

From a hook near the hearth, a cured ham hung. The man cut two fist-sized hunks from it and placed them in a cast iron pan. "I can eat this cold," he said, "but out of consideration for my company, I'll heat it."

"Thank you, sir," she said.

"I take no issue with your calling me *sir*, but I would like you to know that the people in Winchester also name their children."

She got his joke this time, and she smiled, not quite ready to laugh after what she had been through.

And before she could ask, he answered. "My name is Olaudah Moses Davidson."

"Excuse my saying so, sir. But I've never heard that name before."

"You can call me Moses. That is what most people call me." He walked to the shelf and retrieved a paper book. He handed it to her and walked away, tending to the meal. He turned the two pieces of meat with a fork, and the smell of warm ham wafted through the small abode.

"It's good to meet you, Moses," she said, beginning to feel more at ease with him. As unfamiliar as his first name was, his middle name was Moses. And it was an indication that he must have been raised by God-fearing people.

Della looked down at the book in her hand, not sure why he had handed it to her. When she read the title, it dawned on her. *The Interesting Narrative of the Life of Olaudah Equiano.*

"Olaudah," she said, running her finger over the name on the book. "Is he kin to you?" she asked.

"Kindred, but not kin," he told her. "That book belonged to my mother. She named me for him."

Della replied, "He's not someone I've heard of, sir."

"Moses, please," he interrupted.

"Moses, then," she said apologetically. Continuing, she told him, "I've read some, but I've never seen this book." She engaged him out of politeness, but inside all she wanted was to see the boy she loved.

Sensing her disinterest, Moses collected the book from her and carefully placed it back on the shelf. "No, I am sure you have not seen this book, Zebediah from Boone." He removed a piece of ham from the pan, placed it on an earthen plate and handed it to his guest. The other he took for himself and ate out of his hand.

Chapter Twenty-Nine

The home of Ezra and Christabel Hawkins stood stalwart
on the western outskirts of Winchester. It had withstood the
winds of dozens of harsh winters in the mountains. It had seen
snow piled half way up the windows, and the temporary torrents
delivered by summer's hard rain. Strong but unassuming, it
served as a rest stop for many a traveler. Unbigoted, it welcomed
people of all sorts. Black, white, red, Union, and currently a
Confederate named Cumfrey.

The colonial house boasted a large parlor. In better days,
the Hawkins couple often welcomed guests there. But of late,
most of their company was at death's door and in no shape to sit
and converse. And there were currently no happy times to toast.
Albeit a little dusty, the room was still lovely. A blue camelback
sofa lined the largest wall. And four brass sconces, two and two,
regally faced each other casting a warm glow over the entire
space. A woven rug of blues and browns sprawled the length of

the floor--good for keeping the cold out, and for keeping secrets in.

Christabel stood by a window, taking in the morning sunshine. "I can think of no better smell than the smell of ham cooking in the morning," she told her husband. "Moses is a thoughtful host."

"Indeed," her husband replied.

"You would imagine that such a smell would wake anyone," she said.

"Yes, Christabel," he answered.

She went on, "But perhaps it's better that the boy remain sleeping. And be spared the worst of the pain."

"Yes," he answered, dutifully.

"I'm pleased that the other is recovering well," she said.

A moan was heard coming from the upper floor of the house. Without speaking to one another, the husband and wife went quickly to the injured boy. There he lay in a soft, though unfamiliar, bed. Alone and suffering, he cried out. "Where am I?! Cotton?"

Christabel gently touched his face. "You are in Winchester. Don't worry, son." Purposely, she refrained from telling him that he would be *alright*. For she had seen enough war casualties to know that, often, they did not end up alright. And she had seen some perish whose injuries were more slight than these. "Rest now, boy," she said, in a tone she would use with her own children--if the Lord had given her any.

Ezra brought a tin cup, half-filled with some kind of rotgut. And carefully avoiding the hole in his back, the kind lady helped the boy lean up enough to sip it.

"That's horrible," he said, shivering from the taste.

"It will ease your pain," the man told him. "Drink it all."

John did as he was told and lay back down. A feeling of heat spread quickly through his upper body. There was still pain, but not as much. "Thank you," he murmured quietly. "Cotton, Cotton."

"Don't try and talk now, son. You must rest." She stroked his forehead and watched him. When his eyes closed, she began surveying him. There were hopeful signs. His color was good, not that of a dying man. His breathing was steady and strong. Laying one hand on his chest, she felt the heart thumping strong rhythms. She turned to smile at her husband and found that he was gone. Satisfied now that the child was resting, she made her rounds through the big house, down a long hallway and into another room. A smile greeted her as she entered.

"Good Morning, Ma'am," the man said.

"Good Morning, sir." She went to his bedside and pulled the cover from his lower body. "How is your leg today?"

With some difficulty, he shimmied himself upright and answered her. "Better each day."

"I don't believe you'll be walking on it any time soon,"

she told him, removing the old dressing from his wound. "But, thank the Lord, your fever broke and the infection seems to be leaving."

"Yes, Ma'am, I do," he said.

"Good," she said. "Good." She smiled reservedly and added, "I'll return with a new dressing and some victuals."

"Thank you, kind lady," he told her. And, gracefully, she walked away.

The sound of an unfamiliar voice alerted her as she descended the stairway. And she was immediately on guard, uncertain of who might be paying a visit. It was something to which she had grown accustomed. Always something to hide--no matter who came knocking. And Winchester had changed hands so many times during the war, you never knew whether it might be Union or Confederate--or perhaps a once-owned person on a passage to freedom.

Though a proud southerner, Christabel often considered that life seemed easier while the Union controlled the city. But you could never rest on assumptions. She had come across Union who were particularly harsh toward Negroes. And she had come across Confederates who were compassionate toward their plight. So she had long ago decided not to trust anyone until they had proven themselves. For she had learned that people are not always who they seem.

"Christabel, this is Zebediah Cotton. He is the young man

198

who brought John to us," Ezra told his wife.

She politely nodded and smiled.

"Not I," Della said. She looked at Moses. "I'm very grateful to you, sir." Turning her attention back to the lady, she asked, "Can I see him now?"

Christabel was reluctant. "He needs rest. I think it best that we don't disturb him."

"I just need…I mean, I just want to see him. Please," Della implored her.

Mrs. Hawkins affirmed the request with a gracious nod and motioned for the young man to follow. When they came upon the room, Della saw him, flat on his back and eyes closed. A sliver of sunlight shining on his middle.

"He will likely sleep for a while," Christabel said.

Della nodded at her, but quickly returned her gaze toward John.

"The wound through his back is grievous. A large portion of the flesh was gone. It seemed the weapon was close to him."

She replied, "There was no parapet for cover." Images of Diggs and Henry went through Della's mind. And then the thought that they might have done it while she was inflicting justice upon Josiah. A cold and horrible irony. And guilt settled into her heart. The guilt that she was not there for him. Guilt that she did not prevent it. The lady's peaceful voice knocked her out of her daze.

"You have seen him now. He shall rest." She proceeded out of the room, and Della followed. Walking down the steps, Christabel made conversation. "Moses has told me that the Confederacy succeeded in driving the Union northward"

"Yes ma'am," Della responded. We were pressing north, and the yankees were retreating.

"I see," she answered. "I think it prudent for you to remain with us until we know for sure."

Confused by the comment, Della thought before answering. And then it occurred to her. Surely she would be expected to return to service should the Confederates hold Winchester. For John was now in good care, and she was of sound body. What reason could she offer for staying? As far as anyone knew, she was his fellow soldier and nothing more.

"Yes, ma'am," she said. And she found herself hoping that the enemy had prevailed.

"Moses," Christabel said, entering the parlor, "Perhaps Zebediah could stay with you, until we get word from town."

"Of course, Mrs. Hawkins," he said.

She added, "I have much to do, with two men to care for."

"Yes, Ma'am," he said to her, gesturing for Zeb to follow.

Chapter Thirty

"Are you a free man?" Della asked.

"I am as free as you are," Moses answered.

Della did not smile or speak, but instead gave thought to his reply. It crossed her mind that she did not feel very free, stuck beneath a tremendous secret. Unable to express her feelings to the one she loved. "I think, perhaps, you are more free than I am," she told him.

Dumbstruck, he asked, "How so, young man?"

Quickly, she covered herself, "With the war. I am a slave to the Confederacy."

He agreed, "Yes, many are slaves to the Confederacy."

Della nodded, looking down, feeling a little ashamed. "So, you come and go as you please?" she asked.

"I come and go as I please. I do as I wish when I wish. I answer to no human," he stated.

"I've seen some like you fighting in the Union Army,"

she told him.

"I've also seen them." He paused. "Many fled the city when word came about the number of Confederates."

"I don't understand," she said.

"Why would you?" he answered. But he had pity on her ignorance, and elaborated. "A black man is born with enemies. Were you born with enemies, Zebediah?"

Della thought. "The Union is now my enemy. But they were not always."

"I have been engaged in a war since birth. My mother was a smart woman. She taught me to read and write. But there was never a time that there wasn't someone who believed us to be animals. Never a time when we could be sure that no one would apprehend us and enslave us. *That's* a natural enemy. That's a natural enemy like a rabbit is to a wolf." He rubbed his chin in thought. Trying to refrain from harshness, he continued. "Zebediah, how do you suppose your army would treat a black man, a runaway slave, who absconded and took up arms with the Union?"

"Not well, sir," she answered.

In his usual manner, he responded with toned down sarcasm. "No, not well."

Inside the big house, Christabel brought tea and cornbread to the soldier with the injured leg. As he ate, she wiped his wound with warm water and a cloth. He watched her as she tended to him, focused on her purpose. He knew of the husband, but couldn't help himself. For she was a delight to behold. He watched her beautiful pale hands. He watched and felt as she tenderly touched. And, without the help of moonshine, a healing warmth flowed through his body. Just because this woman was close, this woman he knew nothing about--except that she was kind, and beautiful, and married.

"You will be alright, sir," she told him. For she knew that he would mend.

"Yes, kind lady. Thanks to you." He smiled at her. And it was only because he was a Christian man that he did not touch her. For the desire was overwhelming.

"Thank the Lord, sir. It is His work I do." She took his plate and his cup. "I will return at midday."

"Yes, lady. Thank you." He sat and wondered what his fellow soldiers would think. Being sweet on a Confederate woman. The humor got him through his pangs.

The object of his affections once again descended the stairway. She placed the dirty cup and plate into a bucket of water. One clean plate remained in her pantry. On it she placed two big pieces of cornbread. She poured two more cups of tea. Placing it all onto a silver tray, she brought it to the parlor where she rested it on a table.

She pushed aside a lace curtain and peered out the window as if watching for someone. She looked for only a couple of moments and then let the curtain fall. Swiftly, as if she had done it a thousand times, she rolled back the rug, stuck her fingers into a small hole in the floor and pulled hard. A square trap door opened. It wasn't very big, but big enough for a normal-sized human to fit into. She collected the tray and descended into the hole, feet first, one hand on the ladder, and one on the tray.

"It is I," she stated on the way down, trying to ease the minds of her guests. "Not to worry." She planted her feet on the floor and handed them the tray. "I bring food and drink."

"I thank you, Ma'am," the lady said, giving the first piece to her son.

"Thank you," a tiny voice said.

Christabel bent down toward the youngster and hugged him. "You are most welcome, young man." She then addressed the woman. "At nightfall I will bring a meal, and soon after you will go."

The lady nervously nodded, trying hard to appear brave for her child. For, inside she was afraid. But the desire for freedom was greater than her fear.

Moses sat with his own guest not too far away. They had been talking for quite a while. About the war, about the weather, and about other things. Moses talked about his namesake and the suffering that he experienced, the suffering that he witnessed, and the way he won his freedom. He talked about the incredible story and how it had made people think. Made people wonder if slavery might be an evil thing.

Two men on horseback rode toward the home of Moses Davidson. And when he heard them, he began watching his words. In his eyes, Della saw concern, but not panic.

"It's Confederates," he said.

Without thinking, Della ran to the little house, before she could be seen. Moses stayed put and watched them approach his land.

"We're with the Army of the Confederate States of America. We're looking for contraband," one said.

Moses knew what they meant. *Human* contraband. "I am not a soldier, sir," he stated.

"Well, then you must have a master. Where is your master?" he inquired.

Moses had been through this before. And he gave his standard answer. "I'll take you to him, sir." He walked toward the Hawkins home and the soldiers followed.

All the while, Della watched from a window inside the little house. At the big house, the men dismounted their horses and followed Moses to the door. Moses knocked but no answer came. The Confederates grew impatient, imagining that they were being duped. The more aggressive one pushed Moses aside and pounded hard on the door. Startled, Christabel quickly ascended the ladder. While at the top, another hard series of knocks. She closed the hatch and threw the rug haphazardly over it. Just then the door burst open.

Breathing hard but trying to look natural, Christabel pushed her hair out of her eyes and addressed them. "I'm...I'm sorry I was unable to answer, sirs."

They glared at her suspiciously. For they had encountered sympathizers who aided negroes or hid Union snipers in their homes. Even a pretty woman such as this one could not be trusted.

"This man says that this is the home of his master."

"Yes," she told them. "Moses has been with us for many years now."

"Be advised that the Confederacy now occupies this city," they informed her. "We are especially interested in the apprehension of contraband negro soldiers. It is your duty to report to us any knowledge of such activity," they warned.

"Of course, sir," she offered, her breathing finally slowing.

"Good day, then," he said. When leaving, he said to Moses, "Good day to you too, black man."

Chapter Thirty-One

"Now, we're going on a long trip tonight. You and I," the lady said to her little son.

"Yes, Mama," he said to her, almost excited. "Where is it that we're going?," he wondered.

Kneeling before him and holding his face in her hands, she told him, "Now, you don't need to worry 'bout that." She kissed him on the nose. "You let Mama worry 'bout that. We'll be just fine."

"Just fine, Mama," he repeated.

Their meal had been finished and the empty plate sat with two cups on the silver tray. It was a matter of waiting now. And before the morning, God willing, they would be one step closer to freedom. For they were free in the eyes of Mr. Lincoln. But explain that to the slave owners of the south. And even the slaves who had been set free had a whole new set of worries. Put out with nothing into an unfriendly world. No, that was not true freedom. But what she sought for herself and for her youngster would be found in the north, as far north as they could get.

The trap door opened and a familiar voice beckoned in a whisper. "Come. Come you two. It is time."

The lady helped her small son up the ladder before her, and Christabel lifted him out of the top with ease. For he was but three or four and apparently did not eat much. The young mother surfaced a moment later.

Ezra spoke quietly, considering the Confederate soldier in the house, and the one currently with Moses. "Remember this, you are my house servants. And you are accompanying me to Maryland to visit my sister, Clara."

"Yes, sir," the lady acknowledged.

"Yes, sir," the boy repeated.

The man looked at his wife, "We will go now."

She kissed him on the cheek and bade him goodbye. "Godspeed, Ezra." When they disappeared into the night, she prayed, *God temper the wind to the shorn lamb.* She blew out the flickering light of the brass sconces and, except for the light from her candle lamp, darkness blanketed the room.

But a bright glow still burned in the hearth of the little home of Moses Davidson. Realizing that his guest was in no hurry to leave, he had extended an invitation to stay for supper. Cotton obliged. And now the roasted rabbit and boiled cabbage was settling in their bellies.

"It was good. Thank you, Moses." She wiped her mouth with the back of her hand, something she had picked up at bivouac.

"Thank you for the company," he said.

They sat silent for a few minutes while he stoked his fire. It crackled when he pushed a log with the poker. Della let her mind drift into the golden orange glow of the embers. Their heat warmed her face, making her skin feel tight. The light closed her pupils to tiny points, revealing the sparkling blueness of her eyes. Moses noticed.

It was the first night that Della felt like she might sleep peacefully. The first in a long time. And she sat quietly enjoying the fire. Like anyone would do visiting an old friend. Indeed it felt that way. The irony, she thought, taking supper with a black man. Enjoying his company as much as anyone else's--*almost* anyone else's. She thought of John. She thought of his face, his shoulders, his long legs. *How handsome.*

"We've had some lively conversation tonight, Cotton," Moses smiled.

"Yes, we have," she agreed. "Different than most I've heard around the campfires."

Not quite ready to retire, Moses asked, "How so?"

She thought. "The men at bivouac speak often about belching and killing..." She paused for a moment. "And women."

He laughed. "You say that like it's a bad thing!"

Not sure how to respond, she laughed along with him.

"And what do *you* think about women, Cotton?" he requested.

Her jaw hung open and no words came out.

Moses laughed harder. "Cat got your tongue, Cotton?"

She smiled at him, knowing he meant no harm.

When his laughing ended, a breathless Moses posed a question to his guest. "Now, Zebediah." He looked him in the eye. "Do you find me to be a man of my word thus far?"

"Excuse me, sir?" she asked.

"Do you find me to be trustworthy?" He reworded the question.

"Yes, sir," she said, not sure where he was leading.

"I have shared much about myself with you tonight, and I have guarded your secret," he said.

She looked at him, stupefied. "What are you saying?"

He spoke calmly and slowly. "I told no one that you ran when the Confederates came. I could have revealed you. But I did not. Not to Christabel and not to the Confederates. Now, quid pro quo, young man. What can you tell me?"

Della was unsure what *kwid pro kwo* meant, but she understood everything else he said. "What is your inquiry?"

He stated clearly. "My inquiry is this: why did you run when the Confederates came?"

"I can't tell you that," she told him.

Moses pressed. "Are you now a sympathizer? Or have you done something criminal?"

Panic arose in her. *Could he have seen what I did to Josiah?* "I have done nothing that was not just, sir," she stated with conviction.

"And what of your companion?" he inquired.

"What of him?" she asked, growing more uncomfortable.

"Was it he who committed some crime?"

Della was now visibly upset. "No! John Cumfrey did nothing wrong. I'll not have you speak about him that way!" As she shouted, the pitch of her voice climbed.

And it was then that Moses backed off, as if his goal had been accomplished. Calmly, apologetically, he asked, "Now, child, do you have something to confess?" He held his hands out, palms up, like a person does to show that he is unarmed.

Afraid, Della did not speak. What would happen to her if he knew for sure that she was a girl? She kept her mouth shut.

Moses continued gently, "Cotton…whoever you are…I am a man who has experienced much, and who has gained from each experience. The women of my people. Beautiful. Lovely beings. And this I see through the rags that they wear." He stopped, almost exhausted. And when he continued, it was through short breaths, almost begging. "I know not who you are, nor why you are pretending. But I know that my own life has required pretense. You witnessed it. I tell you the truth. I mean no harm, and there is no call for your façade here."

She took a few steps backward to the place where she had slept the night before. She calmly sat herself on the floor. And she cried. The tears of Zebediah's death, of leaving home, of Twila, of the destruction of war all flowed out at once. Sobs bellowed, so much so that Moses thought it might cause a stir. He bent down and put his arms around her.

"It'll be alright, child," he said. "It will be alright."

Chapter Thirty-Two

It had been a week since the Confederates took over the city. And a week since John Cumfrey arrived at the Hawkins home. As thin as he was before, he was even thinner now, kept alive on sips of water and moonshine. And it was time that he eat, lest he die of malnutrition.

Groggy with infection, he was only half aware of Christabel. She rolled him onto his side and cleaned the wound on his back. It was no longer gaping, but completely closed, if only from scabs. The skin around it had become bright red, something to be expected, but not good. To treat it, the gentle lady applied the water of boiled lavender blooms.

"This will help kill the infection," she said.

Not completely cognizant, he was alert enough to tell her, "Thank you."

When she finished, she rolled him carefully onto his back and began working on his chest. For a few days, she had been letting the air hit it, no longer applying bandages. But she remained diligent in keeping the area clean with the lavender water.

"Your breast is healing fine," she said. "It is your back we must watch."

He did not respond, but lay there with dry lips and sweaty head. Christabel wiped his forehead with a wet cloth to cool his fever.

"Here," she said, bringing a cup to his lips. She lifted his head with her other hand and he took a few small sips.

Tasting the fresh water, knowing it was not dreadful moonshine, he quietly said, "More."

Christabel held the cup for him until his thirst was quenched.

"You should eat today," she said to him.

"I'm not hungry," he told her.

"You will eat, for your strength." She gave him no chance to reply, but rose from the bedside and prepared to leave the room adding, "I will be back with some victuals."

In a dream, John walked in the shallows of the James River. By his side, Cotton splashed water at him, and he felt the wetness as if it were real.

Christabel wetted his face. "John," she softly called.

"What, Cotton?" he replied, eyes still closed and dreaming.

"No. It is I, Christabel," she said.

John blinked a few times and gradually regained consciousness. "Ma'am. I'm sorry. I thought you were someone else." And then it dawned on him. "Where is my brigade?" He thought of his friend. "How long have I been here?" he asked.

"Seven days. You have been here seven days, son," she informed him.

"Is there anyone else here with me?"

"No young man. You were brought by another soldier, but he is gone now." She brought the cup to his lips and made him sip.

His body was weak, but his mind now raced. "What was his name?" he asked her.

"Zebediah Cotton," she answered.

"Was he wounded?"

"No, he was not hurt," she replied, purposely giving short answers.

"Where did he go?" John asked, discouraged and feeling abandoned.

"He returned to service in the war." She added, "He might have remained, but the Confederates came and took him. I know not where he is now."

"Oh," he said, his eyes slowly drifting downward.

Christabel retrieved a plate of cornbread from a table and brought it to John's bedside. There she sat, holding the plate as he slowly brought the food to his mouth.

"I can't," he said, nauseated.

"You must."

She cupped his hand in hers and raised it again to his mouth. He took a tiny bite and reluctantly chewed. She offered the cup and he held it himself and slowly sipped.

"That's all. Please." He laid his head back down and closed his eyes. A tear rolled down the side of his face and into his ear.

"Very well, young man," she said. "You have done well for now." She collected the cup and plate and left him to himself.

"He is crestfallen," Christabel told her husband in the parlor. "It will not be good for his healing."

"And how is the other?," Ezra asked her.

"The northerner is well. But he needs to build his strength. His leg is weak with disuse," she explained.

"Perhaps a meeting with the young boy would do good to both of them," Ezra suggested.

"Perhaps. The yankee seems of a kind disposition. And a visitor would do good to the boy's spirit."

He offered a rare complement. "You are a good woman, Christabel."

There was a time when she would have desired more from him, but she grew to be pleased with his scraps of affection, his teases of the romantic love she needed from him. She smiled and took a seat in the parlor for a while. It felt good to just spend some time with him. And she was happy.

Chapter Thirty-Three

Christabel helped the soldier out of his bed. He stumbled and she caught him firmly under the arm.

"I'm sorry, lady," he said to her, embarrassed by his weakness. "It is a sorry man who must be carried by a woman."

"There is no shame in taking help," she told him.

"And from whom do *you* receive help?" he asked. He had seen her do so much even from his sick bed, and never so much a finger lifted by her husband, or anyone else.

"The Lord is my provision," she told him. "I can do nothing without Him."

"You are a good woman," he told her.

She smiled at the floor, but said nothing. Having no crutches, she helped him out of the room and down the hallway.

"I don't recall this part of the house." He looked around, pleased to be upright and out of the too-familiar surroundings.

"You were not well when you came, sir," she reminded

him.

"No. Not well," he said.

Christabel led him into the room and helped him onto a caned chair. "John," she said softly, "there is a visitor."

He opened his eyes, looked, and closed them again. "Please go," he asked.

The yankee looked at Christabel, feeling awkward now.

"John, it is rudeness to treat guests in such a manner." She grabbed him under his shoulders and pulled him half-upright in the bed. "Where would you be were I not hospitable to you?"

"Dead," he said, matter-of-factly.

She sat on his bedside and tipped her head as she spoke. "And *dead* is not a place you should be."

"It *is*," he told her.

Touching his face sweetly, she said, "I will not have that talk, John. Each life is a gift, not something to be cast away." She nodded slowly at the yankee and exited the room.

He understood. Useless for more than a month, he was now assigned a task. And he accepted it eagerly. "John, I cannot walk without help. Therefore I am stuck. When she will come to get me, I do not know. So perhaps we can make the best of this time together. I have been alone for more than a month. But for the kind lady, I have had no visitors. Am I to be rejected by my first company?"

He wanted to be silent, but his kind heart would not allow

it. "No, sir," he said.

"I am Michael Scott."

"You have an accent," John told him.

Michael laughed quietly. "I suppose so. I am not from these parts. Where do you hail from?"

"What does that mean?" he asked, still resistant to the idea of conversation.

"Where are you from?" he said.

"Bladen County, sir," John replied.

"Oh," Michael answered, trying not to roll his eyes. He paused wondering what to say next. "Do you have any family in Bladen County?"

"No," he said. "No one that claims me as theirs."

"I have a sister, and my father," he told him. "They are back home in New York."

Inside, John was flabbergasted. A yankee devil from New York itself right in the same room!

Seeing the look on John's face, the man showed his empty hands saying, "Fear not. I have no weapon."

But John had never been so close to a yankee, and he remained on guard. "I have no weapon either," he said.

"And each of us is currently but a partial man," Michael added, trying to put the boy at ease.

John took the comment his own way. Cotton had gone, and Twila was taken away. Surely, he felt like parts of him had been cut out. He put his hand to his chest and felt the wounds, an outward display of his feelings.

"You rebels are good marksmen," he said, showing John his leg.

"Yes," John replied, still touching his scabs.

Noting the lingering hesitation of his company, Michael said, "You are a man of few words, John." He paused, hoping for a reply. When none came, he said, "Very well, then. I will do the talking. Listen if you will," He told John many things about life in the north. About his hard-working father. About an ill-fated mother. About a desire for a good strong house and lovely wife and children to fill it. He said nothing about the war. Nothing about hatred. And when he had no more to say, he began describing for the boy what he saw out the window.

John lay there wishing that his heart would stop beating. But his apprehension toward the stranger was melting away. For he seemed not a devil, but a man. A man who had experienced triumph, and loss, love, and loneliness. Not a devil at all.

Through the wavy glass, Michael saw Christabel moving about the yard. He watched her as she pulled up vegetables and placed them in a basket. She walked to an apple tree and looked up at the branches. Reaching up, she tipped her head in both directions, looked closely, then plucked the fruit off of the limb and brought it to her mouth. And she did not rest, but kept about her chores as she ate. A pretty young woman arrived and plucked an apple for herself. Michael watched the two in the yard, mixing work and play. He described all that he saw, including the attractive young lass. But all John could think of was the best friend who had slipped away, and the love he had lost.

And outside, Della let her mind wander. She pondered all that she had been through and all that had transpired. Burdock was cold and dead. Josiah Jackson was too. And Diggs and Henry were marching north (toward Gettysburg), having gotten away with their despicable crime. Poor John lay grievously ill. And she was tired of it all. So tired. She had come to see that the pursuit of justice sometimes yields more injustice. For *Vengeance is Mine, sayeth the Lord.* And as for the demon-possessed swine who shot John, only the Lord Himself could repay them now. She finished her apple and resumed pulling weeds.

Chapter Thirty-Four

Another week had passed, and Della settled back into life as a young lady. Refusing to abandon her love, she remained in Winchester, taking a small room in the lower floor of the Hawkins home. With Josiah now gone, she welcomed the resumed identity as if it were fresh and new, thankful to be a girl again. Across the yard, she saw Moses.

"Good Morning, Della."

They walked toward one another.

"How are you, my friend," Moses asked.

"I am well," she replied.

"I am happy to hear it." He smiled at her. "You are awake early."

"Yes, I did not sleep well," she told him. "And Mr. Hawkins made noise in the house. Perhaps he has ridden into town. There is much to do today."

"Much," he agreed. "I shall be working in the yard. I will hear you if you call."

"Thank you, Moses," she said.

He nodded and returned to his home. Looking at the woodpile, he wiped his brow, ready for the sweat. The blade of his axe rested between the fibers of a cut log, and the handle stuck out to the side. He pulled it hard and yanked it free, examining the sharpness. "Good enough," he said, and began his work.

He chopped the wood into pieces small enough for his hearth. When the heat became too much for him, he removed his shirt and resumed raising the hatchet and letting it fall hard. Beads of sweat glistened on his dark skin. A large hunk of tree caught his eye and he paused to examine it more closely, checking it for knots, rot, and signs of weakness. It looked perfect and he set it aside near a stump that he used for sitting.

When he had finished his work, he walked to the chosen wood chunk. He swung his axe hard, splitting it almost exactly in half. Taking another hard swing, he hit it again. The result was a sliver of wood, perhaps three inches in thickness. He hacked off the bark edges and got out his knife. Near the top he carved a small cross. Lovingly, he made it as smooth and as straight as he could. It was the least he could do for the poor girl. She had been through so much. He watched her wandering beneath the trees.

Christabel, too, watched Della from the house. *Poor girl,* she thought to herself. *She seems so lost.* The lady watched for a few moments and then retreated away from the window. She rolled back the rug and opened the hatch in the floor.

"It is I, Christabel," she announced, as usual.

A man and wife sat huddled on the floor with two small children. Christabel collected their empty plates and cups. "Tonight you shall go." She added a warning, "Confederates have been near." She now spoke specifically to the children, bending down to their height. "It is prudent that you be still and be silent on your journey. Whatever happens, be still and silent."

They said nothing, but nodded shyly.

Christabel ascended the ladder, and the hidden lady called to her. "God bless you, Ma'am."

Exercising caution, the kind lady did not reply but continued up the rungs in silence. She put the plates and cups on a table and swiftly returned the room to normal.

The way life had evolved, it was common that the Hawkins home received visitors in both the nighttime and the day. And the normal way of it was this: the darkness brought people of darker skin and, except for Moses, the daylight brought people of paler skin. But whomever was expected, if Christabel Hawkins was not asleep, she was keeping watch.

From her usual window, she observed Moses as he worked. Della bent and touched the object he was crafting.

Their eyes engaged for a second and, in unison, turned in the same direction. Someone approached. Christabel straightened her apron and prepared herself for the typical interrogation. *Is this your black man, Ma'am?* She looked down, making sure that the rug looked normal, then resumed her post at the window.

Whoever was approaching, they were unseen from where she stood. But Moses she saw clearly. He put his hands up in front of himself, like someone does in a stick-up, taking a few steps backward. And it was then that Christabel saw them. Two Confederates on horseback. One with his rifle fixed on Moses.

"Ezra! Ezra!" She ran through the lower floor of the house searching for him. Panic-stricken she retrieved a shotgun from the corner and walked out the door, shaking. Still far from them, she called, her gun poised. "What business do you men have here?!" She continued toward them.

One bound Moses' wrists with rope while the other stormed toward her. Christabel stood her ground in front of him, still trembling. "What business do you have here?!" she demanded. Slamming his hand to her shoulder, he pushed past, knocking her to the rocky ground. He sneered as he marched toward the door, "We'll have no tolerance for sympathizers."

"Della! Find Ezra!" she yelled.

The young girl ran to Christabel and whispered, "He's gone." She then retrieved the shot gun from the ground and ran to Moses and his captor. "You let him go," Della demanded.

"He ain't worth it. Don't get yourself hurt, young lady," the Confederate warned.

"I don't want to shoot you. But I will," she told him, the shotgun pointed downward in front of her.

"Child, don't," Moses said.

The sound of a bang startled them. At Moses' feet, the Confederate lay, not moving. Confused, the three moved quickly.

"Untie him," Della told Christabel. And the girl ran toward the big house, toward whence the shot came.

In the parlor, furniture lay broken and strewn about the floor. Each room had been furiously gone through. And now angry footsteps made their way up the steps to the top floor. Still recovering, the yankee limped away from the window, clumsily reloading his weapon.

"Put it down," a voice ordered.

Michael laid the rifle on his bed and struggled to remain standing. Not completely healed, his leg throbbed. He said nothing but raised his hands in surrender.

"Identify yourself!" the Confederate ordered.

And he complied. "I am Sergeant Michael Scott, Union."

"I got no time for you," he said, and he fired.

Before he could even spit on his enemy's body, the blast of a shotgun sprayed the back of the Confederate's head, and he fell still only feet from his victim.

Frantically, Della ran throughout the entire second floor, screaming, "John! John!" No reply came as she searched each room. Empty. Each bed empty.

Moses walked carefully up the stairs, ready to swing his axe if necessary. "Wait here," he whispered, leaving Christabel shaking in the parlor.

Mrs. Hawkins did as she was told, standing directly over the hatch, thankful that it had not been discovered.

Breathless now, Della ran to Moses. "Where is he?!" she pleaded.

John recognized the voice and called out. "Here. Cotton." Down the hallway, they followed the weak and muffled sound. "Here," they heard again.

For two weeks, Della had feared and lamented. *What would he do when he found out? What would he think when he saw her this way?* Now all that mattered was that he was alive. And she was ready to have him hate her. Ready to face his rejection. For her love was strong. And it almost didn't matter what he thought of her. Almost.

At the end of the hallway, a small door opened up into a storage space where Christabel kept things like candles and blankets. From that place, the voice of John Cumfrey beckoned. Della pulled the door and looked inside. Old quilts placed neatly on the floor. The yankee had taken them out of the box before laying the boy inside. Tapered candles scattered about.

Too weak to push his way out, John called again. "Here. I'm here."

Della knelt down and lifted the top of the box. It was like opening a present. Inside, a face she had missed so deeply. He looked back at her, mesmerized.

Chapter Thirty-Five

Snow fell softly on the Great North Mountain west of Winchester, VA. But fire burned warm inside the cabin. Between the north and the south, war continued. But for Della and John, peace abounded. They wondered how they could have gleaned so much from strife, starvation, death, and bloodshed. And they wondered why they two had been spared.

They were determined to make good use of their lives. So they forgave those who had hurt them, and they loved one another with fierce dedication.

From one solid piece of log, John carved a cradle. He was no longer the skeletal boy of the war. But he had grown strong. He pushed the cradle and watched it rock. It moved smoothly, making hardly a sound. In the afternoon light, his pretty wife sat at a small table near one of two windows. And on this quiet day, as her belly swelled, and there was nothing much to do, she enjoyed the comfort of a warm home and a good husband. For a wedding gift, Moses had given a pen and some ink and a few sheets of paper. She would put it to good use. She watched the deer move gracefully in the snow, and she put down on paper what was on her heart. This is what she wrote.

Dear Momma, I am writing to tell you that I am alive. I pray that you and all my family are well and in the Lord's care. I am married, Momma. But not to who you might think.

The next words will be hard for you to read. But you need to hear them. And I need to say them. It's my fault about Zeb. I have already confessed it to the Lord, and now I confess it to you. It's my fault that Zebediah died. I was there when it happened. It was that awful Josiah Jackson, dear Momma. To you and to my brothers and sister, I am so sorry. I am sorry about Zeb. And I am sorry that I trusted the one who took him.

I've found that life is bitter sweet, Momma. It was through a bloody war and through losing Zeb that I found the one for me. My name is now Della Cumfrey. It's a name I am proud to wear. For my husband is a good man. And were it not for all of the terrible things that happened, I doubt if I would know him. Know that Josiah Jackson has been repaid for his crimes. And I imagine he continues to pay for them somewhere.

I am with child, Momma. You will soon be a grandmother. I pray that you may meet this child someday. My husband and I have decided that if it is a girl, we will name her Twila Rose. And if it is a boy, he will be Zebediah Cotton

Cumfrey. I love you Momma. And I hope that I will see you again in this life.

Mrs. John Cumfrey.

Twila's cross hung over their hearth, a symbol of sacrifice, love, and redemption. And a hand-hewn piece of oak nestled under the snow outside. Beautifully carved by the closest of friends. The lovely cross on top, and the simplicity of one name. The name of a boy who lived his life in Boone, NC. The name of a boy whose end began a journey. A name that would not soon be forgotten. That of Zebediah Thomas Cotton.

For this book and more by Maryann Austin, go to

maryannaustin.blogspot.com or http://maryannaustin.webs.com